"Or are you really afraid that if I kiss you, you'll no longer be able to deny what you feel?"

Natalie guffawed. But she didn't look at him again. She couldn't. She knew that he would see into h___ ___ and know exactly what she was fe___

He relaxed one o___  ___eath her chin, forcing

"That is the most ___

"Is it?"

He held her gaze fo___ ___ beats, the look a challenge in itself. One that said, *Bet you can't look away.*

And darn it, she couldn't.

His finger delicately moved from her chin along the base of her jaw, causing Natalie to suck in a sharp breath. And then, before she knew what was happening, Michael lowered his mouth onto hers.

It wasn't yet the Fourth of July, but Natalie was undeniably feeling sparks. Seeing them explode behind her closed eyelids. The touch of his mouth against hers…had anything ever felt this good?

Why did she feel such a rush of undeniable, insane attraction for this man?

Michael's mouth parted against hers. His sexy full lips felt incredible. And then he suckled her bottom lip, and she felt dizzy from the desire his kiss was awakening in her.

Natalie actually moaned in disappointment when he pulled back, leaving her stunned and speechless. Like someone who had been unexpectedly struck by a flying piece of debris, Natalie stared at him in awe, almost unable to comprehend what had just happened.

His lips curling in the slightest of smiles, he said, "Well?"

Books by Kayla Perrin

Kimani Romance

Island Fantasy
Freefall to Desire
Taste of Desire
Always in My Heart
Surrender My Heart

KAYLA PERRIN

has been writing since the age of thirteen and once entertained the idea of becoming a teacher. Instead, she has become a *USA TODAY* and *Essence* bestselling author of dozens of mainstream and romance novels and has been recognized for her talent, including twice winning Romance Writers of America's Top Ten Favorite Books of the Year Award. She has also won a Career Achievement Award for multicultural romance from *RT Book Reviews*. Kayla lives with her daughter in Ontario, Canada. Visit her at www.KaylaPerrin.com.

Surrender
My Heart

Kayla Perrin

KIMANI™
ROMANCE

For all those who have suffered heartbreak
but haven't given up on love.

 KIMANI PRESS™

ISBN-13: 978-0-373-86260-3

SURRENDER MY HEART

Recycling programs
for this product may
not exist in your area.

Dear Reader,

Welcome to book two of the Harts in Love series!

If you've been in love, chances are you've had your heart broken. Sometimes, we choose someone for superficial reasons, which of course will lead to heartbreak. Other times, we follow our heart and still get hurt. And sometimes, we choose a partner as a way to escape a situation in our lives.

That's what Natalie, the youngest Hart sister, does. Wanting an escape from her past, she hopes that marriage to a man who seems to have it all together will provide her with the happiness and security she craves. But it's only a recipe for disaster.

But even heartbreak gives you a chance to grow and learn. Once you realize that you shouldn't close your heart off to love, that's when you open yourself up to the possibility of real happiness.

Will Natalie take that chance? I'm excited to present her story to you, and I hope you enjoy it!

Happy reading!

Kayla

Chapter 1

Natalie Hart snatched the phone from the wall mount in the kitchen the moment she saw Nigel Williams's name displayed on the caller ID.

"Nigel, thank God," she said without preamble, gripping the phone tightly, desperate for word about her sister's condition. "How is she? How's Callie?"

Nigel sighed wearily before speaking. "She's okay." His voice sounded strained, as if he was trying to be brave. "Patrick Jackson did a number on her—he is lucky I didn't get to him before the Tallahassee police did—but Callie is strong. The doctors say her injuries are mostly superficial and she'll be fine."

"You're sure?" Natalie asked. Yesterday, she had heard the words *beaten* and *concussion* and been terrified. "Because if we need to head down there, Deanna and I will be on the next pl—"

"No, that's not necessary. We won't be here more than another day. By the time you'd get here, you'd have to turn right back around. So it makes more sense for you to wait until we get back to Cleveland."

Deanna, who waited in the kitchen with Natalie, was biting down on her bottom lip and watching her sister closely. "What's he saying?"

"He's says that Callie is going to be okay," Natalie explained. "That we don't have to head to Tallahassee." She paused. "Nigel, are you sure? Because I know Callie might not want us to go out of our way, but we—we're family." Her voice cracked around the word *family,* which suddenly meant so much more now that she and her sisters had reunited. "We need to be there for her."

"Yes, I'm sure," Nigel told her. "I know you're worried, but I wouldn't lie to you about this. If you needed to be here, I'd tell you."

Natalie's shoulders sagged with relief. She believed Nigel, knowing he wouldn't sugarcoat the severity of their sister's injuries.

"What exactly happened?" Deanna asked. She began to pace the small kitchen at Uncle Dave's house, where she and Natalie had been staying since the death of their auntie Jean. "How did this Patrick guy get to Callie in the first place? My God, she could have been killed!"

Nigel, who had clearly heard Deanna's question, said, "That's a story Callie will have to tell. I'm not sure of all the details. But tell Deanna not to worry. I've got it under control. Callie is in good hands. I'm taking her home as soon as I can."

Taking her home... The words caused a small smile to form on Natalie's lips. Just over a month ago, she, Callie and Deanna had returned to Cleveland for their aunt's funeral after being away for several years. The three of them had been estranged for far too long, and sadly it took their aunt's passing to bring them together again.

Auntie Jean's funeral had also led to Callie and Nigel reuniting. Ten years ago, Natalie had been certain that Callie would marry Nigel. It hadn't taken a psychologist to determine that the way they looked at one another proved they had a very deep and special connection.

But then Callie had up and left Cleveland, abandoning her sisters, her aunt and uncle, *and* Nigel. No one had known she was pregnant with Nigel's child at the time, least of all Nigel. Natalie had assumed that Callie had left to get away from her and Deanna, who had been foolishly feuding over a guy. But she'd also had problems of her own and had run to escape them. However, the two of them had never stopped loving each other—no surprise to Natalie—because after so many years apart, they had finally worked out their differences together. Natalie knew it couldn't have been easy, especially not when Nigel felt betrayed at having never known he had a son. But the love between them was still there, and in the end, that love was greater than any of the pain. Now Callie and Nigel were moving forward as a family, not backward. Which was especially wonderful for their son, Kwame, who would now finally have his father in his life.

Natalie couldn't help reflecting on her own marital relationship. While Callie had reunited with her true love, Natalie and her husband of two years had recently split. That special love Callie had found with Nigel was definitely not the kind of love Natalie had found with her cheating husband, Vance.

"Natalie?"

At the sound of Nigel's voice, Natalie realized her mind had drifted. It was hard to stop thoughts of Vance from invading her brain, considering their breakup was still fresh. "Sorry. What were you saying?"

"Just that Callie wants me to make sure you and Deanna don't worry. Patrick Jackson is behind bars, and he won't be going anywhere for a long, long time."

Patrick—the estranged husband of Callie's best friend, Tamara—had retaliated against Callie for trying to help Tamara escape him.

Deanna stopped pacing and extended her hand to Natalie. Despite the reassuring words Natalie had told her, Deanna looked worried to the point of being ill. "Let me talk to him."

Natalie passed her sister the phone. And as Deanna began to speak to Nigel, Natalie took up the job of pacing the kitchen floor as Deanna had been doing.

To say that the last eighteen hours had been nerve-racking was an understatement—learning that Callie had been attacked by a madman in Tallahassee, that she was injured and in hospital. Then making the decision to stay behind to comfort their uncle, who couldn't handle another loss after so recently losing his wife, when all Natalie and Deanna had wanted to do was get to Tallahassee as quickly as possible. The hours that passed were agonizing as they waited for Nigel and Kwame to arrive in Florida so that Nigel could give them an update. Yes, they had heard from Tamara more than once that Callie was in stable condition, but hearing from Nigel would be the much-needed additional confirmation that Callie was going to be all right.

And even still, while Nigel's phone call brought the news they so desperately wanted, hearing their sister was okay wasn't quite the same as seeing with their own eyes.

Perhaps that was a side effect of having a mother walk out of your life and never come back. You needed to see things in order to believe them.

I'll be back for you soon, my darlings. I promise.

But despite their mother's promise, she had never returned.

"Natalie and I don't mind heading down there," Deanna was saying. "In fact, I feel guilty that we didn't. I know our uncle needed us here, but we should be there for Callie, too."

Natalie looked at her sister, who was leaning against the

wall. Deanna wiped a tear from her eye. Natalie understood how she felt. Having lost their mother years ago, and with their auntie Jean dying so recently, neither of them wanted to endure another loss in the family—especially not now when they had just reunited.

"Okay," Deanna said, nodding. "It's just that we're so worried. Callie didn't deserve this. I can't believe anyone would hurt her in this way."

Seeing her sister distressed caused Natalie's stomach to twist as she relived the moment she heard that Callie had been attacked.

But then she said silently, *Callie's alive, Callie's alive,* reminding herself of what was important.

"Well, she should have let the police handle it," Deanna said into the phone. "Wishful thinking, I know. Callie's never been the kind to take a backseat in any situation."

Natalie couldn't help shaking her head. Oh, that sister of hers. Callie was always charging in to save the day. It was a role she played as the oldest sibling, protecting her and Deanna when their mother left them with their auntie Jean that day so long ago. Callie had offered assurances that their mother was okay and would keep her promise. She was fiercely protective of her younger sisters, always stepping in when anyone gave them any hassle.

A smile touched Natalie's lips as she vividly recalled Callie charging up to Allan Cobb the day after he'd snapped the head off of Natalie's favorite doll at school. Callie had pushed the nine-year-old class bully into a puddle of mud in front of a crowd—not caring that it meant a trip to the principal's office. Callie never regretted her actions, because as a result Allan never bothered Natalie again.

As a teen, Callie had joined all kinds of groups to help those in need, and proudly protested against injustice. She wasn't the kind of person who could sit back and do nothing with so much inequality in the world.

From what Natalie understood, Callie's best friend, Tamara, had been in trouble—the woman's possessive ex posed a threat to her life—and Callie had done what came naturally to her. She immediately took a flight to Florida to help her friend, only to find herself in the middle of a domestic dispute.

"So you *really* don't need us to come down there?" Deanna asked.

"Wait a minute," Deanna suddenly said, her tone of voice changing to shock. "What?"

Natalie paused in her pacing to stare at her sister with interest.

"Please tell me you're kidding." Deanna's eyes bulged as she drew in a horrified gasp. "No, Nigel. No…"

"What is it?" Natalie asked. Though her heart was already racing. In the minutes that Nigel had been talking to Deanna, had Callie's situation taken a turn for the worse?

"Rodney Cook," Deanna said, mentioning the name of their mother's ex-boyfriend, the one Miriam Hart had been running from. "Nigel just said that he was stabbed in prison yesterday!"

The words were like a physical blow to Natalie's stomach. Rodney Cook had been stabbed? The one man who could provide the clues that would lead to finding their mother?

"No," Natalie wailed. "God, no. Not after finally locating him! Is he dead?"

Deanna held up a hand to silence Natalie as she listened diligently to what Nigel was saying.

After their auntie Jean's passing, Natalie and her sisters had learned of a letter their aunt had left for them, one that gave all of them hope that their mother was alive somewhere. For Natalie, the letter had proven what she'd always believed in her heart—that their mother wouldn't just up and leave them without a compelling reason.

And it turned out that their mother had left to protect them, because she'd been dating a guy who was involved in criminal activity, someone she had planned to testify against. Testifying against that kind of person could have dire repercussions, not just for the witness, but also for anyone the witness cared about. Miriam knew that Rodney might try to retaliate against her children as a way to punish her, so she had left her children with her sister in order to protect them.

The problem was, Rodney Cook was the only person they knew of who might know their mother's whereabouts and the friends she'd had twenty-three years ago when she'd taken Natalie and her sisters from Cincinnati to Cleveland to stay with their aunt.

"So he's going to be okay?" Deanna asked. "Because he can't die…not before we even have a chance to talk to him!"

Natalie held her breath as she waited for Deanna to say more.

"Thank God," Deanna finally uttered. Then to Natalie she said, "Nigel says Rodney is alive, and they're keeping him in a guarded hospital room. Nigel stressed to the authorities there that Rodney needs to *stay* alive."

Natalie simply nodded, her heart pounding furiously from the moment of fright that their only lead regarding their mother had just been lost.

"All I can say is that it definitely pays to have a cop in the family," Deanna went on. "Maybe we can all head to California to question him."

There was silence, and then Deanna shook her head. "No, of course not. We wouldn't think of going anywhere until you're back with Callie." Deanna paused and her eyes misted. "No, let her get her rest. Tell her we love her and we'll talk to her a bit later. Bye, Nigel."

When Deanna hung up, Natalie went to her sister and took her hands in hers. Her own eyes filled with tears as she squeezed Deanna's hands. "Good Lord, what a crazy twenty-four hours."

"Tell me about it," Deanna agreed.

"But at least the news is good on both fronts. Callie is going to be fine, and it sounds like Rodney will be, too."

"Mercury must be in retrograde," Deanna commented.

"Huh?"

"You know…astrology." When Natalie looked at her blankly, Deanna said, "Forget it."

Ah, that's right, Natalie mused, a memory coming to her. Deanna and her horoscopes. She'd been into astrology as a young teen, always blaming the good or bad in her life on how the planets had aligned.

"The bottom line is, even though bad things happened today, the outcome is still positive," Deanna said. "God was watching out for Callie. And for Rodney."

"Exactly," Natalie agreed. "The positive happened for a reason. It's a sign from above that we have to keep believing. And I believe it, Deanna." Natalie's throat filled with emotion. "We're going to find our mother—after all these years!"

Deanna nodded, but her expression instantly changed from excited to cautious. "I want to believe that, but—"

"Then believe it," Natalie told her. "We can't allow ourselves to think the worst."

For Natalie, Rodney surviving the stabbing was further proof that they would find their mother. She knew that her sisters were more wary in general, fearing that their mother might not be found alive. After all, twenty-three years had passed since she had left them with their aunt. According to Callie, that was enough time for her to come out of hiding, no matter how afraid she was.

Natalie had to believe otherwise, that her mother had good

reason to continue to stay out of their lives. And not because she was cold in a grave somewhere.

She could accept nothing else.

The doorbell rang. Deanna hurried through the kitchen exit, saying, "I'll get it."

Moments later, she said, "Natalie, it's for you."

"Me?" Natalie asked, making her way to the door.

A man in a suit stood on the porch, holding a large envelope and a clipboard. "Are you Natalie Cooper?"

"Yes," she said, tentative.

"I have a delivery for you," he said. "You'll need to sign here."

He handed her the clipboard, indicated where she needed to sign, and Natalie obliged. All the while, she wondered what on earth could have been delivered to her at her aunt and uncle's home.

He took the clipboard, then gave her the envelope. "Have a good day."

And then he was off.

Both Natalie and Deanna watched him get into a dark-colored sedan. Once he'd driven off, Natalie tore open the envelope's seal.

"What was that about?" Deanna asked.

"I'm about to find out." But Natalie had a sneaking suspicion whatever was in the envelope had to do with Vance's text message the previous day. He'd asked for the address of where she was staying so he could send her important mail that had come for her.

She withdrew the papers. "I guess he's filed for divorce," Natalie said, trying to sound nonchalant as her eyes scanned the papers.

But something was wrong. Because while she wasn't a lawyer, she noticed the papers didn't say anything about a divorce *petition*.

Rather, page one of what was undoubtedly a legal document read Decree of Divorce. Now her eyes frantically took in the rest.

"Oh, my God," Natalie uttered. Her insides began to twist violently. Vance had been given an uncontested divorce decree by the state of Nevada.

"What?" Deanna asked.

"Vance…he divorced me."

Deanna made a face. "You mean he's *filed* for divorce."

Natalie handed her sister the papers, then went to the nearby living room and sank onto a sofa.

"But I don't understand," Deanna said after a while. "How could he get a divorce so quickly? And why in Nevada?"

"Obviously you can get rid of your wife in no time in Nevada."

"But you don't live there."

"No." Natalie's mind began connecting the dots that were slowly coming together in her mind. "But we have a house there. Oh, that jerk! He must have used having a home there as a way to claim residency."

Looking confused, Deanna's eyes went over the pages again. A minute later, she spoke. "From what I see here, it looks like Vance claimed he tried to serve you papers but couldn't find you, so the courts granted him an uncontested divorce. However, you are within your rights to contest it, have the case heard before the courts."

Natalie waved a hand. "No."

"But there's property, none of which is mentioned in this agree—"

"I don't care." Natalie dragged a hand over her face. "Vance wants to get rid of me so quickly, let him have it all."

"I used to date a lawyer," Deanna said. "You have rights, sis. Do not let Vance walk all over you."

"I'll be fine," Natalie said. "I have an account that's mine.

He used to give me an allowance—you know, money to go spend on myself shopping or with the other players' wives. I wasn't interested in spending my days acting like the spoiled wife of a basketball player. So I saved what he gave me for a rainy day." She paused. "I guess this is my rainy day."

And then Natalie started to cry.

Deanna sat beside her on the sofa and wrapped an arm around her. "Oh, sis. I'm so sorry."

Natalie turned her face into Deanna's shoulder, taking comfort from her sister as she cried.

Then the profoundness of this moment hit Natalie. Years ago, she had seduced Deanna's boyfriend. That had to led to a ten-year rift between the sisters. Now here was Deanna offering her comfort over a marriage that had fallen apart due to infidelity.

"I'm not crying over Vance," Natalie said through her tears. "Really, I'm not. I guess…I guess I'm just mourning the dream."

And rationally, Natalie knew that was true. Because she had started mourning the loss of her marriage a long time ago. Shortly after she'd said "I do" two years ago, she had sensed that Vance had only married her so she would be eye candy on his arm.

Natalie wasn't a fool. She had the kind of looks that caused men to crash their cars into light poles, she knew that. But she didn't let those looks define her.

And she had hoped that when she'd met superstar basketball player Vance Cooper that he was different—that he had seen past her looks and into her fragile heart.

A heart made fragile because of her mother's abandonment at the tender age of five.

Instead, Vance had become more and more distant after their wedding extravaganza, and Natalie suspected his infidelity within six months of marrying her. So when she had learned that Vance was sleeping with Olivia, her best friend, she hadn't been so much surprised as betrayed.

"I don't think he ever loved me," Natalie said, wiping at her tears.

"He must have," Deanna said. "How could he not? Look at you—you're stunning."

"Looks mean nothing."

"Really?" Deanna countered. "Tell that to all the men who've lost their heads when they've looked at you."

Natalie was certain Deanna was referring at least in part to Marvin, the man Natalie had selfishly seduced over ten years ago. She still wasn't sure why she had hurt her sister like that, except that she had been at a low point in her life, needing to feel alive and desirable.

"Yet here I am," Natalie said, pushing the memory from her mind. "Divorced by a husband who only cared to get rid of me as quickly as he could. Like our mother," Natalie added without thinking.

Deanna eased back so she could look at her. "What do you mean?"

"Maybe Callie is right. Maybe our mother left us because she didn't want us."

"Okay, now I know that's grief talking," Deanna said. "Because out of all of us, you were the one who never stopped believing there was a reason for our mother's disappearance. And now we know there was. So it's not the time to lose hope."

"I know," Natalie said, sniffling. "It's just…I thought Vance respected me more than this."

"Vance is clearly an idiot," Deanna said. "And a coward. I know it hurts, Nat, but trust me when I say there's no point crying over a man who didn't value you. Soon enough, you'll meet the man you're meant to be with."

Now Natalie gave her sister a skeptical look. "What makes you say that?"

"Your horoscope this morning," Deanna answered, her voice filled with certainty. "It said a new love was on the horizon for Scorpios."

Natalie rolled her eyes, but at least she smiled.

"Don't give me that look, sis. You mark my words. You're going to find someone else. It's written in the stars."

Chapter 2

By the next morning, Natalie was in better spirits—despite the front-page news that had confronted her. Wisely, Deanna had taken her downtown to shop at quaint boutique shops in order to take her mind off what had happened with Vance. Retail therapy, her sister had called it, and it was working.

They were currently in a hat shop owned by a local designer, perusing the large selection of funky hats.

"Oh, what about this one?" Natalie asked, taking a wide-brimmed purple hat off of the rack and placing it on her head. "This, with large sunglasses—it'll help me be incognito."

"It'll also cause someone to lose an eye. It's a cute hat, but whoa, could it be any wider?"

"It's exactly what I need," Natalie said. "After that front-page announcement about Vance and Olivia this morning…"

"Eh," Deanna said, throwing up a hand. "We're not going to talk about that, remember?"

"But the front page of the paper here in Cleveland? That's

what I don't understand. Why does anyone here care about my marriage to Vance?"

"Because we used to live here," Deanna supplied. "And you married one of the most successful players in the NBA. But we're not talking about it, remember?"

Not talking about it was a lot easier said than done. Because Natalie could avoid the truth all she wanted, it was still *there*. The magnitude of Vance's betrayal had been published for all the world to read.

But at least this morning, instead of feeling sad as she had the day before, she was feeling anger. Vance had rushed their divorce only to announce the very next day that he and his mistress were engaged.

"All I can say," Natalie went on, "is that they deserve each other. If Olivia is dumb enough to believe that he'll ever be faithful to her…"

Deanna plugged her ears with her fingers. "Not listening to any talk about Vance."

"Okay, I get it. No more Vance talk." Natalie put the purple hat down, then went to something smaller. A cute, casual hat made of straw. "I kind of like this one. It's the perfect summer hat."

"Oh, that is cute," Deanna agreed.

"Here, try it on." Natalie put the hat on her sister's head.

Deanna checked out her reflection in a nearby mirror, and nodded. "Definitely cute."

Natalie took the hat from her sister's head and put it on her own. Looking into the mirror, she nodded. "Yep, this is a keeper."

"If you ask me, she's probably pregnant," Deanna said as she turned and began walking toward another display of hats. "That's my two cents…but I'm not talking about it."

Natalie stopped dead in her tracks. As the reality of what Deanna had said hit her, she felt her stomach roil.

"I'm sorry," Deanna went on, catching Natalie's expression. "I shouldn't have said anything. I'm probably wrong…"

"Actually, you're probably right." Natalie walked past her sister to the window, where something had caught her eye. Some sort of commotion. She saw a woman with a microphone and was instantly worried.

But when she got to the window, she saw that the woman was approaching a tall, gorgeous man who had just stepped out of a black 7 Series BMW with dark, tinted windows.

"What is it?" Deanna asked, coming to stand beside Natalie and also looking out the window.

"I saw a reporter outside. For a minute, I thought…" Her voice trailed off, the idea suddenly seeming stupid to her. "As if I'm that important."

"Ooh, I see you ladies are checking out Michael Jones," came a woman's dreamy voice.

Natalie and Deanna turned to see Edna, the hat designer and shop owner, standing next to them. You would think that the fifty-something redhead had been hit by Cupid's arrow, that's how enamored she looked.

And for a long moment, Natalie allowed herself to enjoy the view of one of the finest men she had seen in ages. Tall, at least six foot three, with a cool confidence that oozed sex appeal. Black slacks covered a seriously fit behind, and hugged thighs that were muscular and strong. His well-sculpted biceps were revealed beneath the hem of his expensive-looking short-sleeved shirt. Having been married to Vance Cooper, Natalie recognized high-priced clothing even without seeing a label. And from the man's fine Italian shoes to his dark sunglasses, everything on Michael's body was undoubtedly created by a renowned designer.

Natalie cleared her throat and said, "I wasn't checking him out." She pretended to be intrigued by a felt pink cowgirl hat. "Just wondering what was with the reporter."

"That's probably just a random woman with a store-bought microphone, hoping to get close to Michael," the shop owner said with a giggle. "Michael Jones is one of the star's of this city's NFL team, and women do anything to get to him. Wide receiver. Very talented."

Of course, Natalie thought, wondering how she hadn't pegged him as a professional athlete. *I'm sure he's very talented in many ways,* was her next sour thought.

"He comes by here quite often, because he's got a restaurant a few doors over," the designer went on. "A soul food place. Bought it for his cousin to run, and unlike some of those other stuck-up athletes, he drops by a lot. It thrills the fans."

"I'm sure," Natalie quipped. Then she promptly turned around. The brother was fine...no doubt about it...but she was in no mood to ogle a professional athlete.

"Sorry to talk your ear off," Edna said. "I'll leave you to your shopping. I guess I'm as guilty as all the other women in this town. When Michael Jones comes around, I have to get a glimpse."

"I can see why," Deanna said.

Edna shrugged sheepishly, then added, "I'm here if you need any help."

"We're good," Natalie told her. Moving away from the window, she saw another interesting hat. She picked up the baseball styled cap adorned with gems and glitter. The word *love* was written in glitter, which only made Natalie think about Vance again.

"Pregnant," she mumbled to herself. "My God, it makes sense."

"I was only speculating," Deanna said. "Which was really silly. Because without any pr—"

"I don't know why I'm surprised," Natalie went on, as though Deanna had just confirmed that she had heard rumors

Olivia was pregnant. "Seriously, I shouldn't be surprised. Vance is capable of anything."

"Me and my big mouth," Deanna said. "This is exactly why I didn't want to talk about Vance. You're only getting more upset."

"How can I not be upset? Why else would Vance divorce me without even the courtesy of letting me know ahead of time? Obviously because he got that tramp pregnant."

"That hat I like," Deanna said, trying to change the subject. "Yeah, real different."

"I'm taking it." Natalie walked back to the large purple one and picked that up, as well. Then she picked up a white cloth hat she hadn't even tried on and walked with the items toward the front register.

"Lovely choices," the designer told her. "Now, I don't know if you had a chance to see the fascinators I have in this corner. Those are the little hats that rest on the front of your head. They became real popular after the royal wedding. A lot of ladies are wearing them to church. They're not nearly as hot in the summer. The one with the blue feathers is made from the feathers of my friend's tiger macaw—"

"I'll take it," Natalie said. "And give me that black fancy one with the jewels and netting."

"Where are you going to wear that?" Deanna asked in a low tone.

"Oh, I don't know. Maybe Vance's funeral?"

"Oh, boy," Deanna said.

"Did you say you're going to a funeral?" Edna asked, her face twisting with concern.

"My aunt recently passed," Deanna quickly said before Natalie could speak. "My sister was saying this would have been a nice fascinator to wear to the funeral."

"Or any funeral," Natalie added.

Not that she wished Vance dead.

Well, not particularly. She didn't plan to participate in a voodoo ritual to ensure his painful demise.

The purchases paid for, Deanna all but hustled Natalie out of the store. "Retail therapy is over. I say we go home, and you get into a hot bath—"

"Natalie Cooper?"

At the sound of her name, Natalie instinctively turned. It took her a moment to recognize that the woman moving toward her was the same one who had earlier approached Michael Jones. Natalie's eyes went lower, to the microphone the woman had in her hand.

"How do you feel about the news that your barely ex-husband has just gotten engaged?"

Natalie was too stupefied to speak.

"You *did* hear, didn't you?" the woman asked, sounding almost gleeful. "The ink is barely dry on your divorce papers, yet Vance has already proposed to Olivia Markson. From what I understand, she was your former best friend, right?"

"Don't you have anything better to do?" Deanna asked, stepping in front of Natalie.

"Please don't sensationalize this story," Natalie said. "No one in Cleveland cares about me and Vance."

"But the people of San Antonio most certainly do."

"San Antonio?" Natalie asked, not understanding.

"I'm sorry. I should have introduced myself. I'm Hyacinth Hamilton, from the *San Antonio Times*."

A reporter from San Antonio was *here?* A reporter had tracked her down in her uncle's hometown? Natalie glanced around nervously, wondering if there were more reporters lurking nearby. When she and Vance had announced their separation two months ago, the reporters had converged like vultures.

"So how do you feel about what's transpired?" the reporter went on.

"I—I—" Natalie's head was spinning. God help her, she didn't want another media spectacle made of her life. Hounded wherever she went...

"You didn't know," the reporter surmised.

"Of course she knew," Deanna snapped, "but she doesn't care. Now, if you'll leave my sister alone."

"Deanna Hart," the reporter said, grinning as though she was a little star struck. "When will you come out with a new CD? Your fans have been waiting for what, nearly three years now?"

"Leave us alone," Deanna reiterated, sounding sterner, and Natalie couldn't help thinking that Hyacinth had hit a nerve.

Deanna took Natalie by the arm and hurried in the opposite direction toward where the car was parked. Natalie almost made it there, but stopped and turned. It hit her suddenly, the severity of Vance's betrayal. And Olivia's. The ink wasn't even dry on the separation papers, much less the divorce papers. And already Vance was moving on?

How dare the two of them so publicly flaunt their adulterous relationship at that hotel in Vegas, where Vance had presented Olivia with a huge diamond. According to this morning's paper, witnesses had heard Vance tell Olivia that he loved her "more than anyone he had ever loved in his life."

"Here's what I have to say," Natalie began as she reached Hyacinth. "Vance and I are divorced. He's free to do what he likes. And as far as I'm concerned, he and Olivia deserve each other. I won't take a guess as to how long their marriage will last, but you know what they say about cheaters. In any case, I couldn't care less about the two of them because I've *moved on,*" she finished with finality.

Then she whirled around—and bumped smack into the hard wall of a masculine chest.

"Excuse me—"

"I'm sorry—"

Natalie slowly looked up. The silk shirt she had seen earlier. The sleek sunglasses.

Michael Jones put his hands on her shoulders to steady her. And then a slow grin formed on his perfectly full lips as he looked down at her.

"I'm sorry," Natalie repeated.

Michael's eyes swept over her, leaving her skin feeling flushed. Or was that the Cleveland sun?

"No need to be sorry," Michael said in a voice that was deep and smooth. He sank his teeth into his bottom lip before speaking. "In fact, I am the exact opposite of sorry. Sweetheart, you can bump into me any time, any day, any hour."

I get it, Natalie thought, and stopped herself from rolling her eyes. "All the same, I apologize. I wasn't looking where I was going."

She sidestepped him and began to walk toward the car, and was surprised when Michael took her hand. "Oh, no," he said. "I can't have you walking away from me, not when fate had us meet. What's your name, sweetheart?"

Natalie didn't speak, just checked out the smile he likely thought could charm any woman into his bed.

"Angel?" he guessed when Natalie stayed silent. "Yeah, I bet you looked just like a little angel when you were born, and that's what your mama named you."

Now Natalie did roll her eyes. Wow, the guy really did think he was smooth.

"All that matters," she began calmly, "is that I know *your* name, Michael Jones." She smiled. "You have yourself a good day."

Natalie slipped her hand from his and jogged this time, hurrying to the car where Deanna was waiting.

"What does that mean?" Michael called out to her. "Come on, sweetheart—you really gonna walk away from me like that?"

"What's going on?" Deanna asked when Natalie got into the car.

"Drive," Natalie said. "Now."

For the rest of that day and into the next, the news of Vance's engagement was the talk of all the gossip shows. Like Deanna had speculated, others wondered if Vance had gotten a quickie divorce from Natalie because Olivia was pregnant.

Natalie had tried to put all the gossip out of her mind, painful as it was. For some reason, it helped to think of her brief encounter with Michael Jones. The quick moment of flirtation, one-sided though it had been. Natalie enjoyed remembering that sexy smile on Michael's face, so quickly followed by his surprised expression when she'd walked away from him.

Athletes. They were a different breed. Rejecting him had given Natalie a momentary surge of power at a time when she had been feeling powerless.

It had also been wonderful to see Callie, Nigel and Kwame upon their return from Tallahassee the previous evening. Natalie had been able to forget about Vance as she spent time with her newly engaged sister, fussing over her injuries like a mother hen and oohing over the beautiful engagement ring Nigel had presented to her. It had been a happy evening, one in which Natalie's personal life had been firmly put on the back burner.

But later that night, as Natalie lay in bed alone, she hadn't been able to get past what Vance had done. And though she didn't care to hear another word about the man she now considered the biggest mistake in her life, she couldn't help going to the website for the *San Antonio Times* the next day after breakfast to check out what Hyacinth had written.

I'VE MOVED ON, VANCE'S JILTED WIFE INSISTS

Natalie groaned as she saw the headline on the first page

of the paper's website. If that was the headline, what would the article itself say?

Natalie scrolled down. There was a wedding photo of her and Vance that had been graphically altered to look like a picture being ripped down the middle. Juxtaposing that photo was one of Vance and Olivia cozying up at a blackjack table in Vegas, looking like the happiest couple in the world.

Natalie wanted to throw up.

She didn't care to read the article. It was too much. Breaking up was hard enough, but doing so in the public eye was unbearable.

Maybe Deanna was right about that whole Mercury in retrograde stuff. Because each day was bringing more stress. Yes, Natalie had been on a high after learning that Callie would be fine, and seeing her last night had been wonderful indeed. But it was hard to escape the reality that the person she'd married for life had so little disregard for her that he would divorce her quickly in Nevada, only to flaunt his engagement to her former best friend.

Natalie turned off the computer and went into the bathroom opposite her bedroom on the second floor of her uncle's home. She didn't want to wallow in the misery of wondering if Vance had ever loved her, because it ultimately didn't matter. But yes, the truth was that she absolutely had hoped for the fairy tale with her husband.

She locked the bathroom door, then turned on the shower. A nice, hot shower was what she needed to push thoughts of Vance out of her mind.

"You want me to break his legs?" Callie had asked last night as they'd all been at Nigel's home. "Because I'll do it. As soon as my injuries heal, I'll head to San Antonio and take care of him."

That had gotten laughs from everyone, including Natalie, who at the time had been able to compartmentalize her pain.

Concentrating on the reality that her sister was alive and well was far more important than the fact that she had lost a man who had not loved her.

At least that was what she had told herself yesterday. But now…Natalie swallowed a sigh. And as she stepped into the hot shower, she began to cry again.

Angry with herself, she slammed her hand against the tile wall. "Save your tears, Natalie. Just because you always believed in fairy tales doesn't mean you're childish enough not to accept that when something is wrong, it's wrong."

And marrying Vance had been wrong. She hadn't known it at the time, but people made mistakes in this life. They were supposed to learn from those mistakes and move on. At least she knew she had done her part to keep the marriage going—which included being faithful to her husband. She had wanted forever with Vance. He, however, had been so into himself and the fact that he was the great Vance Cooper that he couldn't truly care for another person.

With that thought, Natalie allowed the hot water to splash over her entire face. And she hoped that as her tears mixed with the water and disappeared down the drain, so would the remnants of anything she felt for the man she had been fool enough to marry.

Chapter 3

Natalie was seasoning boneless chicken breasts to grill for dinner when the phone rang *again*.

Deanna, who was in the kitchen with her cutting potatoes for the salad, was the one who went to answer the phone.

"Maybe you shouldn't answer it," Natalie said. "I'm sure it's another reporter." Another reporter who clearly wanted to hear her bad-mouth Vance so he or she could feed the team of hungry tabloids and gossip magazines with more dirt.

They had been calling since the sun had come up, and frustrated, Natalie had stupidly spoken to a reporter just after lunch. The woman had wanted her response to the fact that Vance was talking up a storm about how he had found his "true love" and how that made her feel. It was the kind of ridiculous question quack reporters were famous for: *Your son was just crushed by truck. How do you feel, sir?* Natalie had hung up without answering.

"If it's a reporter, I'll get rid of the pest," Deanna said.

"But maybe it isn't, because this time the display isn't showing that a private number is calling. It's a Cleveland number."

"That doesn't mean anything," Natalie pointed out. She would never forget the time someone had come to her house pretending to be an electrician, when, in fact, the man had been a reporter trying to get the scoop on whether or not Vance was actually considering leaving San Antonio to play for a Los Angeles team.

Reporters would do anything to get the story they wanted.

Picking up the phone, Deanna uttered a pleasant greeting then paused. "Are you a reporter? Okay, then may I ask who's calling?"

Lowering the phone and covering the mouthpiece with her hand, Deanna said, "Natalie, it's for you. Some woman named Penelope who claims she's not a reporter."

Natalie narrowed her eyes in suspicion. "You don't actually expect her to say, 'Yeah, I'm a reporter.' Come on, Dee."

"She said she's from some children's charity," Deanna explained.

Natalie frowned, but was slightly less suspicious. She did a lot of charitable work in San Antonio. But still she said, "Ask her what charity."

Deanna put the phone to her ear again. "What charity?" And after a moment, "Oh. Okay."

"Well?" Natalie asked. She knew some of these reporters were very clever. She didn't want to be tricked.

"She says it's a local children's charity for kids with cancer, and she could really use your help. That she knows of your charitable work in San Antonio." Deanna shrugged. "I don't know. She sounds legit."

It was a subject near and dear to her heart, one Natalie had spent a lot of time lending her voice to back in San Antonio. But still, it could be a trick, a desperate reporter who knew enough about her to try and lure her onto the line under false pretenses.

"Are you going to take the call?" Deanna asked, still covering the mouthpiece with her hand.

"All right." Natalie supposed she may as well talk to the person on the phone, even if she would only end up telling the woman off for her ruse. She turned on the kitchen sink, washed her hands, dried them with a dish towel, then crossed the kitchen and took the phone from her sister's hands.

"This is Natalie Cooper. I mean Hart." If Vance was already engaged to somebody else, then why should Natalie use his surname anymore? She was a Hart. And it was even more important for her to cling to that connection to her mother now, to her sisters. The Hart name had much more meaning to Natalie at this point in her life than it ever had before.

"Hello, Mrs. Cooper," came the relieved reply. "I'm really glad I found you."

"And who are you?" Natalie asked, knowing that she sounded a little brusque.

"My name is Penelope Rand. And I knew your aunt. Jean... she was such a wonderful person. She gave so much to this community, volunteering for one cause after another. I really appreciated her and I miss her terribly."

Thinking of her aunt caused Natalie's chest to tighten. "Yes, I miss her, too."

"I was excited to hear that you are in town, especially because your aunt told me about your efforts to help raise funds for childhood cancer research. I'm on the board of a small local charity, Compassion for Families, and our mandate is a little different than what you're used to. We don't raise funds for cancer research. Rather, the money we raise supports a home here in Cleveland where families from out of town can live while their child is undergoing treatment at one of the local hospitals. Or, if they live in town but are facing financial hardships because of the cost of medical care, we help out with rent or mortgage payments. The cancer patient needs support, but so does the entire family unit—and that's where we come in."

"That's wonderful," Natalie said.

"We're currently working on putting a gala event together to raise funds. It's very last minute, but we need to pull this off because Compassion House needs urgent financial help or it'll have to close its doors. With the economy's current shape, there have been less donations and between trying to help keep people in their own homes, there isn't currently enough to keep the house running at the level we'd like. I don't have to tell you how devastating it would be for families from out of town to suddenly have nowhere to go. So we were hoping to have an event within a six-week timeframe, possibly less. I don't know how long you're in town, but if there's any chance you could help out, lend your vast expertise to the cause, that would be amazing."

That's how to get them, Natalie thought. *Compliment them, and how can a person say no?* It was one of her strategies for helping to elicit funds and favors from people when she worked at getting financial support to help a certain cause.

"I'm not sure how long I'll be here, either," Natalie told her. "I mean, the cause sounds great, absolutely. It's definitely something I would support. But I'm just in town because of my aunt's passing, and to spend some time with my uncle and family. Since I'm not even certain how much longer I'm going to be staying here, it wouldn't make sense for me to make a commitment. You're going to need someone who can give one hundred ten percent of their time. But I'll happily—"

"I would take whatever time you're able to give," Penelope said quickly, and Natalie heard a hint of desperation in the woman's voice. "It's been hard to garner support. The economy is in rough shape, people just don't have the same kind of money they used to. And when they do donate, they give to bigger charities. But if I could have someone high profile like yourself, with your connection to your husband, Vance Cooper—"

"We're not together anymore," Natalie said, swallowing the lump that had lodged in her throat at the mention of his name.

"I know," Penelope said, sounding contrite. "I heard about your split. And I'm sorry. But, you're still very well connected. Your husband…ex-husband…is a successful NBA player. He has a wealth of friends who are very successful, and who know other successful people. Any connection to them that you may have can be of assistance."

Natalie nodded. "I understand. I do. But I just don't want to bite off more than I can chew right now. The last thing I would want to do is disappoint you and your organization. Any project I take on, I like to see it through to the end. And right now, I just can't say that I could do that for you. But I'll definitely make a substantial donation to your charity to help with your immediate needs."

"Oh, I'm certain you would do a fantastic job," Penelope insisted. "It's not simply the fundraising we need help with. I hate to say it, but I'm not that experienced with throwing the kind of posh event I'm hoping to pull off. The organization is small, so there aren't that many of us on the board. But I feel forever indebted to Compassion For Families because of my own personal story and am compelled to help them in every way possible. My seven-year-old son is a cancer survivor. Three years ago, when I needed this house—after losing everything to put toward my son's medical care—I don't know where I would have been without Compassion for Families. What I'm saying is that I'm not some expert event planner. I'm just a woman who cares because I know how much this charity means, how important it is."

Natalie said nothing. What could she say? Telling this

woman no—after she had poured her heart out—was almost impossible to do.

"I've made some calls," Penelope went on. "And the prices to hire a person to pull off an event like this are quite frankly astronomical. More than the organization can afford right now. But I do have a connection to one of the players on Cleveland's NFL team—he went to school with me. He said he would be happy to help out. And when I heard you were in town—and knowing how giving and loving your aunt was—I thought it wouldn't hurt to reach out to you, as well. With two celebrities heading up this event, I think we can pull it off and raise more money than ever."

The woman was making it harder and harder for Natalie to say no. But she wasn't ready to commit. Not with Callie injured, and her uncle still grieving, and knowing the kind of time commitment an event like this required. So she said, "I do appreciate the fact that you're even considering me. I'm quite honored. And as I said, the cause is clearly worthy and one that is near to my own heart, as well. But how about I think about it, let you know?"

Penelope emitted a little sigh. "That's the best I can hope for, that you'll consider it. I do hope you will let me know soon."

"Definitely," Natalie said.

Penelope then gave Natalie her home and cell numbers. "I'll await your call, then."

"Sure. I'll let you know either way." Natalie had always hated waiting for a response from someone and hearing nothing. "There may be some other way that I can help out, even if I can't commit to seeing this fundraiser through to its end."

"Great. I'll talk to you soon."

All Natalie could think about the rest of that day and all through the night was Penelope's call. Penelope had made a great point—that the money people gave to charity often went to the bigger, older, more established organizations.

The truth was, Natalie knew how to fundraise. She had made it her life's mission in San Antonio. How could she not offer her help to Compassion for Families?

Besides, she was going nowhere soon. With Vance and Olivia now engaged—and shacking up together in the home she'd shared with Vance for all she knew—where was she going to go? Back to San Antonio, where she would no doubt suffer more media scrutiny? No, it only made sense for her to lie low in Cleveland until the story about her and Vance's marriage finally died down.

Not to mention the fact that she wanted to be in town in order to continue the search for her mother with her sisters.

That fact had sealed the deal, and by the next morning, Natalie had made her decision. While she expected and hoped to put one hundred percent of her time and effort into finding clues that would lead to her mother, it certainly wouldn't hurt to spend some time helping Penelope with her fundraising efforts. The truth was, event planning came easy to Natalie, because she had done it so often. And as Penelope had said, athletes and athletes' wives and other people in high-profile positions were able to get tasks done more efficiently, simply because they had connections to people who had more financial resources.

After breakfast, Natalie called Penelope.

"Natalie?" Penelope said without preamble.

"Yes, Penelope. It's me."

"You've made a decision?"

"I have," Natalie said, and paused. "I really love what you told me about Compassion for Families and I'm more than happy to help out."

"Excellent!" Penelope exclaimed. "And timing couldn't be more perfect. Remember I told you about the football player friend of mine who is also going to be helping me with this cause? Well, he's coming into our office today, and this would be a great chance for you to come and meet him. In fact, he's on his way right now. Why don't you come to the meeting? With the gala date only six weeks away, there's no time to spare in getting started."

"You want me to come in now?" Natalie asked with hesitation.

"Unless you have another obligation right now."

"No, I'm free now," Natalie decided. There was no real reason she couldn't head in to the office and meet this man she would be working with. As Penelope had said, there wasn't a moment to spare.

"Excellent! Let me give you the address, and I'll see you soon."

Natalie scribbled the address on a piece of paper. "I'm on my way."

"I can't wait for you to meet Mike Jones," Penelope added.

Natalie's stomach lurched at the mention of the name. "I'm sorry. What did you say?"

"Mike Jones is the football player I was talking about. My friend from school. He's a sweetheart, and real easy on the eyes. You'll like him."

Suddenly, Natalie's brain was scrambling to try to come up with a reason to do a one-eighty and tell Penelope that she could no longer meet her, no longer volunteer her time.

Yeah, I bet you looked just like a little angel when you were born, and that's what your mama named you.

"As in Michael Jones?" Natalie asked for clarification.

"Yes, that's him," Penelope said. "Oh, you know him?"

Natalie's hands tightened on the receiver as she closed her eyes. "No. I've just…heard of him."

"Excellent." Penelope couldn't sound more pleased. "All right. See you soon."

Chapter 4

The entire drive to the Compassion for Families offices, Natalie felt as if she had a bowling ball sitting in her stomach. At least ten times she contemplated—and dismissed—the idea of turning around and heading back home.

How silly are you being? she asked herself as she parked beside a sleek BMW. *What—are you incapable of working in a professional capacity with a man like Michael Jones?*

That was the thought that had her getting out of her car and making her way up the steps of a large, older home with a wraparound porch. Clearly, this was not only the home where the families in need resided, but also the building that held the charity's offices.

Natalie drew in a breath as she stood before the door, then reminding herself that she was acting like a schoolgirl, she opened it.

She was immediately greeted by a woman who had to be Penelope—a five foot nothing African-American female with a short afro, light brown skin and a sprinkling of freckles on her nose.

"Natalie Hart," the woman said, extending her hand. "I'm Penelope Rand. So nice to meet you."

"Nice to meet you, as well," Natalie said. Then she looked beyond Penelope, in the direction of a woman who was crossing the far end of the hall with a tray of cupcakes.

Penelope turned to follow Natalie's line of sight. "That's Cynthia. She's one of our staff members. She bakes the most extraordinary desserts."

"The house certainly smells lovely," Natalie said.

"Would you like a cupcake?" Penelope asked.

"No, I'm fine." Natalie waved off the suggestion. "Leave them for the children."

"All right, then. This way." Penelope gestured to the door on the immediate right.

Natalie started into the room—and stopped dead in her tracks. Though she had known she would see Michael Jones in the room, laying her eyes on him again was like a shock to her system.

Good Lord, the man was so…

"I know, I'm sorry the office is so cluttered," Penelope said, mistaking the reason for Natalie's hesitation. "Please bear with the mess."

"It's fine," Natalie said, avoiding looking directly at Michael. But as she put one foot deliberately before the other and walked farther into the room, she could feel Michael's gaze on her.

His eyes were burning her skin. She felt flushed and didn't know why. And strangely, she found her breathing had become shallow.

Embarrassment, she told herself. *That's what it is.* And she knew that was true. After yesterday—

"I've cleared space at the end of the conference table," Penelope explained, jarring Natalie from her thoughts about the day before. Penelope began walking toward the table, and as Natalie feared, she took a seat opposite Michael, which left Natalie one option—to sit beside him.

"Michael Jones, this is Natalie Cooper—I mean Hart. Natalie, this is Michael Jones, the local football player I was telling you about."

"Pleasure to see you again," Michael said, eyeing her up and down as if she were a juicy steak.

"Oh, I'm sorry," Penelope said, her expression one of confusion as she took a seat opposite them. "I didn't realize that you knew each other."

"We don't," Natalie said.

To that, Michael raised an eyebrow. "Actually, we met yesterday."

"Briefly," Natalie clarified. "A chance encounter on the street."

Natalie sat and pulled her chair in, trying her best to ignore the uncomfortable sensation that came from knowing that Michael wasn't taking his eyes off of her.

"She's right," Michael agreed. "We didn't enjoy the pleasure of a formal meeting." He extended his hand to her. "I'm Michael Jones."

Natalie turned to face him, knowing that it would look suspicious if she didn't. And she saw that the edges of Michael's full lips were twitching. He was trying not to smile. Clearly, he was enjoying having the unlikely upper hand. Yesterday, she had thought she would be rid of him forever when she walked away from him on the street, and yet here he was, in her life again.

But Natalie couldn't hardly let him know that he was getting to her on any level, so she took his hand and shook it. "Nice to meet you, Michael," she said, keeping her voice dispassionate.

"*Very* nice to meet you."

Natalie swallowed—hard. She felt a rush of heat. That bedroom voice, those sexy eyes…why on earth was he getting to her? It wasn't as if she hadn't seen an attractive man before.

But Michael Jones wasn't simply attractive. He was *hot*.

He's a block of ice, you're a block of ice, Natalie said mentally, trying to trick herself. Because no matter how hot this man was, the last thing she wanted to do was look twice at another professional athlete.

Least of all look twice at one who was giving her the bedroom eye as though he hoped to make her his next conquest.

Nope, Natalie had learned her lesson the first time around, and would not be foolish enough to make the same mistake twice.

What was the saying? Fool me once, shame on you. Fool me twice, shame on me.

Not that Michael had ever fooled her, but she had already been fooled by his species: the professional athlete. Women threw themselves at men like him. Stalked them at their away games. Tried to sneak into their hotel rooms. Got hired as wait staff where they ate their meals. Natalie knew all the tricks. Heck, Vance had joked about the various ploys of these women, making Natalie believe he was immune to their charms. And yet Vance had betrayed her, despite his vows to love, cherish and be faithful.

She supposed it was only inevitable that men like Vance cheated. A man was only human, after all, and how long could he realistically resist temptation when it was always in his face?

Penelope cleared her throat, and when Natalie looked at her, she was horrified to see a knowing smirk on the woman's face—the kind of smirk that said she believed Natalie had just been checking Michael out.

"I checked out your charity on the internet," Natalie said,

needing to say *something* to get Penelope's mind off of the track it was clearly on. "I'm really impressed. For a small charity, you have been able to do incredible work."

"And we hope to continue to do that work," Penelope said. "Which is why both of you are here."

Natalie nodded. Then, despite herself, she glanced at Michael again, and saw that his gaze was still intent on her. It was the kind of gaze that left a woman feeling totally exposed.

She jerked her head away. She could already tell that this Michael character was the type of guy used to getting what he wanted. First of all, he was gorgeous. Certainly not the kind of guy most women would kick out of the bed in the morning. Add that to the fact that he was a successful athlete, and he was all but irresistible to most women.

The way Michael kept checking her out made it obvious to Natalie that he thought all he had to do was give her a dose of his smoldering looks and his dazzling smile and she would be putty in his hands.

"Now, the date for the gala event is August 12," Penelope said. "Which gives us just about six weeks. Unlike some of the events we've done before, this will be a celebrity event. I would like both of you to be cohosts for the event. I've seen video of you on the internet, Natalie, and you're a natural with a microphone. And of course, you are, too, Mike," she added amiably. "With the two of you headlining the event, we're sure to have a great turnout."

"What exactly do you mean by headlining?" Natalie asked. "Do you want us to emcee, or provide some sort of entertainment?"

"Oh, no, I don't expect you to be the entertainment—unless of course you have some jokes you'd like to share—but your job will be to host," Penelope explained. "You're both celebrities, you both speak well. You'll emcee the evening, introduce each new segment for the night, be it the auction items or the various entertainment."

Natalie nodded. "Gotcha."

The phone rang, but Penelope stayed seated at the conference table, not getting up to go to the desk and answer it. "I'm working on some of the entertainment as we speak." Penelope spoke over the ringing phone. "I've made some calls to a comedian, a local church choir, a popular dance troupe and some others. So far, only the gospel choir has confirmed, but I'm hopeful the others will, as well."

"We'll follow up with whomever you've reached out to," Michael said.

"Excellent," Penelope said. "I'm sure that hearing from both of you will inspire people to say yes. I want a real high-class event that will justify the cost of the ticket price."

"You know, I could ask my sister if she'll perform," Natalie said. "Deanna Hart."

Penelope's eyes lit up. "Oh, yes, please do. That would be fantastic. I didn't know if I should ask, given that you all are grieving, but having her on the lineup would be amazing. I love her music. She has such a beautiful voice."

Natalie felt a pinch of pride. Though Deanna wouldn't know it, Natalie had bought the three CDs she'd put out over the past eight years. She may not have been speaking to her sister at the time, but she had been proud of her success nonetheless.

"I've got some musician friends I could talk to, as well," Michael said. "I'm sure they'd be happy to lend their support."

"And speaking of dancers," Natalie began, "I have a friend in San Antonio who is a very talented ballet dancer. She leaves audiences breathless, seriously. I can give her a call."

Penelope's wide grin indicated not only the woman's happiness, but her relief. "I knew you both were the perfect ones for the job. I'm so glad I ran into you, Michael, because that gave me the idea to have celebrities headline this event. This is going to be our most successful event ever, I just know it!"

"I wouldn't say I'm a celebrity," Natalie said sheepishly. Her only claim to fame was having been married to Vance Cooper.

"Of course you're a celebrity," Penelope said. "Athletes' wives are famous, too—especially ones who grew up in Cleveland. And with the amount of charitable work you do, you're also good people."

Natalie smiled. "Thank you."

The phone rang again. Penelope sighed. "I really ought to get that."

"No problem," Michael said, rising from his seat. "You've got a lot to do. I think Natalie and I should take it from here, sit down and brainstorm and then get back to you."

Penelope held up a finger as she hurried to the phone. She answered it and asked the person on the other end of the line to wait for a moment.

Then she returned to the table, where she handed Natalie and Michael a folder each. "I need to take this phone call. But these are my initial plans, which the two of you can peruse. Have a gander, brainstorm together and we'll talk at a future date."

"Oh, sure." Natalie stood and accepted Penelope's proffered hand. But she was suddenly out of sorts. She wasn't thrilled about the idea of her and Michael having to spend time together alone. She would prefer to do the planning with Penelope involved.

Michael shook Penelope's hand, and then turned to Natalie when Penelope went back to the phone.

"Why don't we talk outside?" he suggested in a low voice, careful not to speak too loudly and disturb Penelope.

"Sure," Natalie agreed.

Michael gestured for her to walk in front of him, so she

left the office first. Getting to the double front doors moments later, Natalie reached for the right handle. But her hand collided with Michael's as he reached to do the same thing.

"Allow me," Michael said.

Natalie drew in a deep breath. The touch of Michael's hand against her skin, the deep timbre of his voice…he was doing this on purpose. *Trying* to see if he could get to her.

But she said nothing, just stepped onto the porch, where the heat of the late-June day enveloped her. But that was nothing compared to the heat she saw smoldering in Michael's eyes when she turned around and looked up at him.

"So," he said.

Natalie's pulse picked up speed—and then she felt disgusted with herself. Good Lord, what was wrong with her? Why was this man getting to her on any level? So what if he was seriously fine, with a body chiseled to perfection?

Obviously Natalie needed a distraction from the reality of Vance and his betrayal—but seriously, Michael Jones? There couldn't be a worse man to feel even a remote attraction to.

Natalie cleared her throat and averted her gaze. "I'll take a look at Penelope's plans, you do the same and let's talk in a couple of days. Give me your card, and I'll call you."

"Actually, I was thinking more like dinner. Tonight."

"Dinner?" She narrowed her eyes at him. A beat passed. Then another. Then Michael's lips curved in a smile.

Natalie couldn't believe his gall. "Are you seriously asking me out on a date?"

Michael's eyes crinkled with amusement. "Actually, I was suggesting we have dinner in order to discuss some ideas for this fundraiser. But if you want to make it a romantic date…"

Natalie swallowed, feeling foolish. "Oh."

"How about seven o'clock? Right where we met on the street yesterday. I have a restaurant there, A Taste of Soul.

We can meet there. Have a relaxing meal. Enjoy some Dixieland jazz."

Though it shouldn't have, Natalie's heart began to beat a little faster. Michael had said this wasn't a romantic date, but what he was describing certainly sounded like it. Natalie could only imagine his plan of attack: feed her a delicious meal, give her a few drinks, allow the music to set the mood, then suggest that they head back to his place.

She had fallen for that game once before. She wouldn't again.

"We can speak over the phone," she told him. "I think we should at least look over Penelope's plans separately before we come together to discuss ideas."

"Trying to run away from me again?"

Natalie's right eyebrow shot up. "Excuse me? I just presented you with a practical plan. How on earth did you deduce—"

"All that matters is that I know *your* name," Michael said, and it took Natalie a moment to realize that he was quoting her words from yesterday. "I have to say, I don't think I've ever been rejected quite like that before."

So that's what this was about. "I see I bruised your ego—"

"Ouch—"

"Which wasn't my intent," she continued. "So for that, I apologize." She began to dig through her purse. Staying here and engaging Michael in more chitchat was getting them nowhere. "But like I said, I'd like time to peruse Penelope's plans before we get together. Here's my card—"

"Tonight. Dinner. You'll love the soul food. Southern fried chicken, collard greens…"

"On second thought, it's probably best that the next meeting be with both of us and Penelope," Natalie said, not liking where this was going. She put the card back into her purse.

"Let's both touch base with her in a couple of days and then schedule the next meeting."

And then, before Michael could say a word, Natalie started down the front steps of the house. She needed to get away from him. Natalie knew his type, and wasn't going to entertain his "I'm not flirting" flirtation any longer.

She hurried around the side of the building, not looking backward. She knew she was doing the same thing she had done yesterday—running from Michael, as he had said. Natalie wasn't naïve, and she certainly wasn't born yesterday. No matter what Michael said, it was clear that he had designs on her, and the last thing she wanted to do was lead him on in any way. So going out to dinner with him to discuss the charity even was a definite no-no.

At least not tonight. Let her go over Penelope's initial plans on her own, then she and Michael would talk. That way, their next interaction would truly feel like a business meeting as opposed to a date.

But as Natalie rounded her car to the driver's-side door, she stopped in her tracks. Silently, she cursed.

Because her grand plan of escape had totally been destroyed.

She had a flat tire.

Chapter 5

"What the heck?" Natalie asked as her eyes took in the sight of the front driver's-side tire. "How in God's name?"

"Need some help?"

Natalie spun around and stared at Michael. Her first thought was that he must have somehow been behind this. But she knew he couldn't have been. He had been in Penelope's office with her for their entire meeting. Had been in that office even before Natalie had arrived.

"What?" Michael asked, his eyes narrowing with speculation. "You can't seriously think I had anything to do with this?"

Natalie didn't answer the question. She wanted to blame him for this inconvenience, because it meant having to spend even more time with the man when she wanted nothing more than to get away from him. She wasn't certain why she was so desperate to escape him, only that she was.

"Looks like I have a flat tire." Vance had always told her

that she wasn't good at assessing a car's needs, only at driving one. She hadn't needed to be, not when her high-end Mercedes had indicated to her whenever the car needed something. But now that she thought about it, the rental car had felt a little off. It had seemed a little lower on the left side as she had been driving earlier. But she had paid no particular attention, figuring that was no big deal.

Clearly, however, the tire had been losing air.

"If you pop the trunk," Michael began, "there should be a spare. I can help put it on."

"There's no need for that," Natalie said.

Michael raised an eyebrow. "Is that so? Does that mean you're one of those women who knows how to change a tire?" The look he gave her—sizing up her designer heels and her delicate flowery dress—said he didn't believe that she would be capable of changing a tire. At least not in that outfit.

Natalie wanted to tell him that she was perfectly capable of changing a car tire, and she would almost be tempted to spend the hours required to do the job just to send him on his way. But she said, "I'm going to call the rental car company. They can send someone to fix the tire."

"There's no need for that," Michael told her. "I can do it."

"You're not exactly dressed for tire changing, either," Natalie pointed out, taking in his dark jeans and black cotton dress shirt, also noting yet again just how fine his body was.

"Better me get dirty than you."

So the man was chivalrous, something Natalie appreciated. Still, she said, "You'll put a spare on, but I'll still have to deal with the issue of the problem tire being replaced."

"And you can deal with that once you're at home," Michael told her. "Wouldn't that be preferable to waiting around here for the rental car people to show up?"

Michael had her, and he knew it. If she protested anymore—

"Unless the reason you don't want me to help is because you're afraid to spend any time with me."

Natalie's mouth fell open in shock. She made a sound of derision. "Excuse me?"

"You heard me. Seems to me that just like yesterday, you want to get away from me as fast as you can. But it's also clear to me—as became evident when you walked in the door earlier today—that fate is making sure we spend time together. So I say why fight it? Just roll with it."

Natalie began to pace, her heels crunching on the gravel. This totally sucked. Anything she said to counter his argument would come off as defensive, and she truly had no reason to be defensive with Michael. And yet he was absolutely right—she didn't want to spend any time with him. If she could go back on her word and say no to helping out with the fundraiser, she would almost consider that. Simply because the idea of spending more time with Michael was extremely unnerving.

"Why don't you just give me your keys?" Michael told her. "If you don't, you're going to give me a complex," he added with a smile.

Reluctantly, Natalie passed him the keys to the Chevrolet Cruze. Crossing her arms over her chest, she watched as he opened the trunk.

After rummaging around in the trunk for a couple of minutes, Michael turned to her and said, "There's a spare tire here, but I don't see a jack. Which doesn't make sense. One should be here."

"And you're sure there isn't?"

Michael nodded. "And I don't have one in my car."

"It's okay. I am perfectly happy to call the rental car company. Let them deal with this. They're going to need to know about the flat, anyway."

Michael nodded. "Okay. I guess that makes the most sense."

Inwardly, Natalie beamed. Finally, he would be on his merry way.

"Why don't I take you to my restaurant?" Michael suggested. "You can wait there. Instead of dinner, we'll take a look at the plans together over lunch."

"That is completely unnecessary," Natalie said. "I'll stay here with the car. Wait in the building."

"You're going to wait here? Why would you do that? You can kill two birds with one stone—enjoy a great meal and discuss the fundraiser."

"I'm not hungry," Natalie said, and heard her stomach grumble at that unfortunate moment.

"Pardon me? I'm not sure I heard you correctly?" Michael said, grinning as though he knew he had won this battle.

"Okay," Natalie said, knowing that she sounded exasperated but unable to help it. Nothing was going her way today. "I'll call the car rental car company, and find out how long it will take them to get someone here. Then we can go to your restaurant—since you are clearly going to think I'm avoiding you if I dare to say no."

Michael's smirk grew, his silent way of saying that that was exactly what he thought.

"We'll go over the plans, brainstorm some other ideas. But I just want to make it clear that our meeting is strictly about the charity."

"What else would it be about?" Michael asked.

Natalie gave him a pointed look. "You may be right about the fact that I was trying to avoid spending time alone with you—I'll give you that. But that's because I can tell you are interested in…in something *more*. I'm not a fool, Michael."

"I didn't say you were."

"Good." Natalie exhaled sharply. "Perhaps I was taking

the childish way out by trying to run away from what I saw as an advance on your part, but now I'll be direct. You need to know that I'm at a place in my life where I am *definitely* not looking for a relationship. I know that men like you are not used to having women say no to them, but I am saying no."

"I didn't ask."

"Well, whenever you were going to get around to it," Natalie said sternly. "The answer will be no if you ask me today, tomorrow or next year. So don't even bother. Got it?"

"Got it," Michael said, but he still looked amused.

Feeling flustered beyond belief, Natalie opened up the glove compartment and retrieved the rental car company agreement, then made the call. To her dismay, she learned that it was going to take about an hour for someone from the company to arrive.

A thought came to her. "Is it possible for me to get picked up at a different location?" she asked. "A friend has suggested lunch at a restaurant called A Taste of Soul."

"That's not necessary," Michael said. "I'll give you a ride back to your car."

Natalie held up a hand to quiet him. "Oh, good. You know where it is. If you can pick me up there, that'd be great."

"I can give you a ride," Michael reiterated.

"Yes," Natalie went on. "Have the person coming call me when he—or she," she added, throwing Michael a pointed look, "gets to the restaurant. Excellent."

Then she ended the call.

"That wasn't necessary," Michael said. "I could have driven you back."

"It's going to take them an hour to send someone," Natalie told him. *Far too long.*

"At least that will give us time to have a decent lunch," Michael said.

"Fine," Natalie mumbled. "Let's do this."

"Seriously," Michael said, "no need to stress out. This is just lunch. A chance to brainstorm. Don't you think it's better to brainstorm with someone else, as opposed to alone?"

Natalie stared at him, wondering if that was a subtle come-on. Or perhaps she was reading too much into it. She had just laid out the ground rules, which Michael had accepted.

And then he smiled, and damn if Natalie didn't feel flushed again. Especially when her eyes went lower and caught a glimpse of his muscular chest.

This is ridiculous, she told herself. Why should she feel anything when she looked at Michael?

"You seem unsure," Michael said.

Natalie knew that Michael was right—her tension was obvious—and given that she had told him she wasn't ready for a relationship, she figured she may as well tell him the reason she was so uptight. "I'm sorry if I've been testy," Natalie began. "I'm sure you probably heard that I was married to Vance Cooper. And unless you've been living under a rock, you must have heard about his affair and our very recent divorce."

"Yeah, I did."

"You may be the nicest guy in the world, but I know what athletes are like. I was married to one. So I can't allow myself to be suckered in by a sexy smile or an attractive face."

"Ouch." Michael placed both hands over his heart, as if wounded.

"Not trying to be harsh, just keeping it real."

"I heard it, I get it. Strictly business." Michael smiled, letting her know that he wasn't annoyed. "You ready for lunch now? Because you'll love the shrimp gumbo, guaranteed."

Natalie headed toward Michael's BMW, not looking at him because she knew she had just made a tactical error. She had gone on and on about how she wasn't interested in a relationship and how things needed to be strictly business when he hadn't even officially hit on her.

Which, she now realized, might make Michael believe the exact opposite of what she'd said. That instead of being un-interested, that she most definitely was.

Chapter 6

A Taste of Soul was a beautiful establishment that Natalie guessed could seat around two hundred people. She had expected to see a shrine to Michael Jones—she had seen that sort of thing at other restaurants owned by athletes—but she was pleasantly surprised. There were photos of staff members and various celebrities who had dined here on the walls, and yes, some with Michael and the chef and other staff. But this restaurant clearly wasn't an ego-booster for Michael in the way Natalie had imagined it might be.

"Hey, Mike," an attractive woman greeted them as Michael led the way to a booth in the back of the restaurant.

"Afternoon, Diana."

Diana smiled politely at Natalie, but Michael didn't introduce them.

"Is that your cousin?" Natalie asked. "I heard you bought this restaurant for your cousin," she explained when he looked over his shoulder at her.

"My cousin's wife." He paused at a large booth, then gestured for Natalie to sit.

Natalie took a seat, looking around as she did. The restaurant was a mix of rich mahogany wood and vibrant reds, offset by cream-colored walls. Near where she was seated was a stage area, which must be where the nightly entertainment performed.

"It's really a lovely restaurant," Natalie said. "Even though it's large, it's got a homey feel. Not to mention it smells incredible."

"They're just getting ready for the lunch crowd," Michael said as he put his car keys and folder on the table. "Which hits capacity at around twelve-thirty."

There were only about eight people in the restaurant right now, but it was only eleven-thirty. "Does it typically get full for lunch?"

"Every day of the week," Michael said.

He was still standing, forcing Natalie to look at his incredible body as she met his gaze. Okay, so no one was putting a gun to her head, but it was hard to ignore his beautiful physique when she was eye level to his midsection and not his face.

"What can I get you to drink?"

"A soda's fine. Gingerale?"

"Sure. And you want the gumbo?"

"Why not?"

Michael disappeared, and Natalie forced herself not to turn and watch him walk away. Instead, she nervously focused on her fingernails. "I could use a manicure," she thought to herself.

She soon became bored with looking at her hands and shifted her gaze to Michael's keys. Not that she meant to spy on him, but she noted there was a photo on the key chain, and could see the long black hair of a female.

Curious, Natalie lifted the key chain and checked out the picture.

She had expected to see the smiling face of some gorgeous female, but instead, the photo was of a young girl. Definitely beautiful, but this certainly wasn't the picture of a woman that Michael would be romantically involved with.

Not that it should matter to Natalie in the least.

"One gingerale."

At the sound of Michael's voice, Natalie quickly tossed his keys. But she tossed them too far, because they went flying off of the table and onto the seat opposite her.

"Sorry," she quickly said, feeling like a kid who had been caught with a hand in the cookie jar. "I just…I saw the picture and…" She swallowed. "She's a beautiful girl."

"My niece," Michael explained. He placed two glasses of gingerale on the table.

"I'm sorry," Natalie repeated. "I don't know what got into me."

There was that amused look again, which made Natalie's heart beat faster. "No problem. You were curious about me. That's allowed."

Natalie dug her nails into her palm. Sheesh, that was the last thing she wanted Michael thinking. Changing the subject, she said, "I thought you were getting the gumbo."

"It's not quite ready. Diana will bring it out in a few minutes."

Michael took a seat beside her, and Natalie couldn't have felt more uncomfortable. She quickly reached for her drink and took a sip.

Michael opened up the folder and began to peruse its contents. Natalie quickly lifted her own folder from the seat beside her and did the same thing.

"These notes are pretty basic," she said. "Names of people she'd like to perform. Ideas for silent auction. Hmm."

"What are you thinking?" Michael asked her.

"I'm thinking that other than the date, we'll be planning this from the ground up."

"Not enough time?" Michael asked.

"It's a tight deadline, but I've worked with tighter," Natalie said. In fact, some of her best work had been done when there had been a deadline crunch and no room for error.

"She's got a lot of names on this list, a lot of performers and artists she has yet to confirm with. If you think we need to tell her to push the date back—"

"No, it's doable." Besides, Natalie wasn't sure how long she was going to stay in Cleveland, and pushing the date further back would only extend the time frame of her obligation to be here. "In fact, with the timeline being tighter, maybe it's better. That way, we can stress the urgency of people committing immediately."

"Sounds like you know your stuff."

Natalie glanced at Michael. "I've done this a time or two."

"I trust you."

"We'll need to get posters and other promotional items for the event done as soon as possible. Which means we'll need to finalize the main entertainment acts. If we could nail down four, that'd be good. So we need to figure out which performers will be the most high-profile and do our best to secure them. I'm sure my sister will say yes." Natalie took a pen from her purse and wrote her sister's name on the paper, then circled it. Looking at Michael she asked, "You're more familiar with Cleveland and who's hot here. Who else should we try to secure first and foremost?"

"The Faith Gospel Choir, definitely. They're amazing."

"Okay." Natalie put a dash beside that name and added, *Call immediately.*

"I know a couple of musicians, as well," Michael said. "More than a couple, really. Your sister is an R&B singer, so how do you feel about having a rap group? I went to school with two of the guys in InEffect, a local group. They rap a cappella—the human beat box, all those incredible sounds. I swear, it sounds like someone is playing an instrument. I'm sure we can count on them to say yes."

"Sounds wonderful," Natalie said.

Diana appeared with a tray holding two steaming bowls of gumbo and a basket of steaming corn bread. "My cousin didn't introduce us," she said as she put a bowl on the table in front of Natalie. "But my name is Diana."

"Hello, Diana. I'm Natalie C—" She stopped herself abruptly. "Natalie Hart."

"Yes, I know." Diana put a bowl of gumbo in front of Michael, giving him a look of reproof as she did. Then the look turned to intrigue—the kind a person gives someone when they think they're on a date with a new love interest.

"We're working on an event for the Compassion for Families charity," Natalie felt compelled to say.

"I don't know how Michael does it, but he always ends up working with the pretty ladies," she said, then winked at Michael before she turned and headed away.

Natalie looked over her shoulder at the woman, wondering what that wink was about. Had Michael told her something in the kitchen?

It didn't matter. Whether Michael had told her something, or whether he had gotten sexually involved with every other female he'd ever worked with, it didn't matter. There were going to be no extra *perks* to their working relationship.

"What?" Michael asked.

"Nothing," Natalie replied, wondering if he was picking up on her thoughts.

"You going to try the gumbo?"

"Definitely." Natalie dipped her spoon into the delicious smelling soup and tasted the gumbo. And then her eyes grew wide as she savored the flavor. "Oh, my goodness. This is delicious."

"I told you."

Natalie then picked up a piece of the corn bread, added a dollop of butter and tasted it. "Light, fluffy. This has got to be the best corn bread I've ever had. No wonder you say the place fills up for lunch every day."

"Glad you like it."

"I'm glad you suggested lunch." Natalie offered Michael a smile, and realized in that moment that she had forgotten about her initial discomfort about spending time with him. She had feared that Michael would turn into a smooth-talking playboy who would make an unwanted advance, but instead, he was being nothing but pleasant.

So what if he was an athlete who was easy on the eyes? It had been her own nerves and speculation that had caused her discomfort, not his behavior.

"This is truly tasty," Natalie said, then continued to eat. She felt foolish for initially rejecting the idea of lunch, given that this was one of the best meals she'd had in a while.

Between bites, she said, "We're going to have to get on the calling part right away. You'll call InEffect, and I'll of course talk to my sister. But we need to narrow down who will call the other people."

"Mmm-hmm."

Natalie took another mouthful of gumbo, then looked at the list in the folder. "There's a good page and a half of names." Beside each name, Penelope had listed what she wanted the person or people to do. "Why don't I take over the first half of the list? I'll call up until…" Natalie scanned the list, then stopped at the name Pastor Calvin Browne. "Until Pastor Browne. You call everyone after that."

"All right."

"We won't be able to use everybody, but at least we can

determine who'll be availa—" Natalie stopped short when her phone rang. Glancing at the screen, she saw a Cleveland number that she didn't recognize, and figured it was someone from the rental car company.

Putting the phone to her ear she said, "This is Natalie Hart."

"Mrs. Hart, hi. I'm Jeff. I'm supposed to replace your car's flat."

"Yes, great."

"I'm outside the restaurant, ready to pick you up."

"Oh, okay. That was fast."

"Is he here?" Michael mouthed.

Natalie began to rise. "I'll be right out."

"But what about your gumbo?" Michael asked when she hung up. "You didn't even finish half of it."

"And it was so good." Despite herself, Natalie regretted that Jeff had arrived already. "But I—I've got to go."

Michael got up, as well. "At least let me give you a to-go container."

"You don't need to—"

"It's no problem."

Michael hustled off with her unfinished bowl, and Natalie couldn't help checking out his magnificent form. The way his muscles moved beneath his shirt…Michael Jones was seriously sexy.

Reminding herself that she didn't care if he was the most gorgeous man ever created, she gathered her belongings. Then she headed to the front of the restaurant, where she stood in front of the hostess stand to wait for Michael.

He joined her a minute later carrying a brown paper bag. "One order of gumbo and some fresh, hot corn bread," Michael told her as he handed her the to-go bag.

"Thanks so much."

Their fingers collided as Natalie accepted the bag, and

her eyes flew to Michael's. His fingers lingered on hers, and Natalie found herself momentarily transfixed by his gaze.

Michael raised an eyebrow in a suggestive manner. "Any time you want to do that romantic dinner…"

Natalie took a sudden step backward. "Of course."

"What?"

"Here I thought you weren't going to make an advance," she said, wondering how she had so easily been drawn in by his sex appeal. "But you just couldn't stop yourself, could you?"

"What can I say? All that talk about us being strictly business and how you weren't going to be sucked in by an attractive face…it was kind of sexy." Michael flashed his charming smile. "And hey, at least I know you think I'm attractive. That's a start."

"No, it's not. You completely missed the point."

"It can be about business, and a little pleasure," Michael said.

"Oh, my God. You are totally not hearing me."

"You're a very beautiful lady. Can't blame me for wanting to get to know you."

Natalie made a face. "I'm sure there is no shortage of beautiful women in your life."

Michael chuckled. "Oh, really?"

"Most definitely. A ball player like you? You've got them all on speed dial."

"Wow," Michael said, seeming more amused than offended. "You've got me all figured out, huh?"

Natalie's chest began to tighten. She didn't want to be having this conversation. "I have to go."

"Yeah, of course you do."

Natalie shot a quick look over her shoulder at Michael as she hurried to the front door. He met her eyes with a steady gaze. It unnerved her.

"We'll talk later," she said, and quickly walked through the door.

"How we gonna do that?" Michael asked. "You haven't even given me your number."

Natalie ignored him and approached the man who had to be Jeff, relieved when Michael didn't say another word.

Michael stood outside of the restaurant, watching as Natalie escaped into the white Ford rental car with a tall, lanky blond guy. He couldn't help smiling to himself. He was more intrigued by her rejection than put off. Michael had been raised mostly around women, had dated his fair share of the finer sex, and he had a pretty good idea how to read them.

And what he was reading where Natalie was concerned was that she was definitely attracted to him.

He could see it in the shallow breaths she'd been taking every time their eyes connected, the way she had fidgeted with those beautiful hands. Not to mention the way she had hardly been able to hold his gaze.

Either she was used to being hit on—which he wouldn't doubt, given her beauty—or she'd made sure to tell him she wasn't interested before he'd hit on her because she was fighting her own attraction for him.

No matter the reason, Michael was looking forward to seeing Natalie again.

Very much so.

Chapter 7

"Sis, are you listening to me?"

Natalie jerked her gaze to Callie, who sat opposite her in the living room in Nigel's home. She and her sisters were having some girl time while Nigel was at work and Kwame was next door at his friend's place. She had zoned out, once again thinking of the way she had all but run for her life when Michael had asked her out for a romantic date yesterday.

And thinking of the way the man had haunted her dream last night.

Natalie had awoken flushed, alarmed to realize that she had been dreaming of him. In her dream, instead of hurrying away from him as she had the day before, she had let him wrap his arms around her and plant a hot kiss on her in the middle of the street for all the world to see. It was as his hands had smoothed over her bottom and his mouth moved to her neck that Natalie had been jarred awake.

Maybe she was simply feeling bad for walking away from

him in the manner she had. Had hurrying away from him when he'd said that he would need her phone number been a totally childish thing to do?

"Natalie?" Callie said, with a chuckle. "You look like your thoughts are a million miles away."

"I'm sorry," Natalie said. "What were you saying?"

"I was asking what you think about the idea of Nigel going to California alone?" Callie said. "I really wanted to go, and I know both of you did, as well…but he made a compelling argument that we should let him handle this. I think he's right. Maybe one person—a cop—is the best one for the job. He'll be able to be objective in a way that we can't be."

"Wow," Deanna said. "I can't believe the day has come when you're willing to step back and let someone else take the lead."

"Touché," Callie said. "But, if getting attacked by an enraged madman taught me anything, it's that I can't solve all the world's problems. Not that I wouldn't do the same thing again—"

"A leopard can't change its spots," Natalie chimed.

"—but this is one of the times when it's okay to let someone else take the lead. My fiancé knows how to handle this."

Deanna beamed. "*Fiancé.* You're enjoying saying that, aren't you?"

Callie's smile lit up the entire room. "Yeah." She extended her left hand and stared at her diamond solitaire engagement ring. "I am."

Natalie's stomach tightened, and she drew in a deep breath. She was happy for her sister, but the idea of any wedding, given that hers had crashed and burned, made her feel… regret. Not that she was missing Vance, but it was still hard for her to deal with the fact that she had married a man who clearly hadn't loved her.

"When's the big day?" Natalie asked, doing her best to keep her voice light.

"We were thinking of maybe a Christmas wedding," Callie replied. "Something small. It doesn't have to be a big affair."

"Oh, but it should be a big affair," Deanna protested. "It'll be the first marriage for both of you. One that should have happened years ago. So you've got to go big."

A big, lavish wedding. The kind Natalie had had. It was most definitely the kind of wedding Callie and Nigel deserved.

"I'm sorry," Callie suddenly said.

"Why?" Natalie asked.

"Because here I am going on about a wedding, being totally insensitive to your situation."

Natalie waved off the concern. "It is what it is. I don't want to take away any of your joy. You and Nigel waited a very long time to get back together. Vance and I…well, we weren't supposed to be together in the first place."

"Hey," Deanna began in a gentle tone, "you'll find someone else. A man who will truly adore you."

At the words, an image of the sexy Michael Jones entered Natalie's brain. And then she scowled. Why she should be thinking of him at this moment, given her sister's comments, made no sense.

The truth was that she had been thinking about him even as she visited with Callie. Remembering his easy smile…and his suggestion that they go for dinner. A part of her couldn't believe his gall at using their working together as an opportunity to hit on her. But another part of her was…

No. She tossed the thought from her head. *I am* not *intrigued by his interest.* Okay, maybe she was flattered, especially given the fact that Vance had dumped her for her best friend, but she wasn't *intrigued.*

"Absolutely you'll find someone special," Callie agreed.

"That won't be for a long, long time." Natalie forced a smile. "I think I'm through trusting men."

"Until you meet one like Nigel," Callie couldn't help saying with a breathy sigh.

"Okay, okay, I get it," Natalie said, and rolled her eyes playfully. "You are sickeningly happy—" Grinning, she got up from the sofa and took the steps toward where Callie was sitting in the recliner, and gave her sister a kiss on the forehead. "And I couldn't be happier for you."

"Thanks, Nat."

Natalie sat back down. "So when is Nigel planning to head to California?"

"Probably next week. He's in court this week for a murder trial, but expects it to wrap up soon."

Natalie nodded. "Another week. All right. We can deal with that."

"Plus, it'll give Rodney time to heal," Callie went on. "That way he'll be in good shape for Nigel's questions."

"Good point," Deanna agreed. "And we've waited this long for answers, it won't hurt to wait another week."

"I guess not," Natalie said. Though she was anxious for the search for their mother to continue. In the meantime, however, she had the charity event to concentrate on.

"Dee said you're volunteering with a local charity," Callie said, as if reading her thoughts.

"Yeah. Compassion for Families. They run a house where out-of-town families can stay while their children undergo treatment for cancer. Or if they're local, the charity helps with mortgage or rent payments so that the burden of medical care doesn't force folks from their homes."

"That's wonderful," Callie said.

"It's going to be a big event full of great entertainment. Including our own sister." Natalie looked at Deanna.

"I'm happy to do it," Deanna began, "but I'm not sure why they want me."

"Hey," Callie said. "Don't say that. You're an amazing artist."

Deanna shrugged. "One who was dropped by her record label."

"What?" Natalie asked. "Why?"

Deanna shook her head, making it clear she didn't want to answer the question.

"Well, whatever the reason," Natalie began, "that doesn't take away from your talent. Penelope from the charity was elated when I said I'd ask you to perform."

"Well, thank you," Deanna said. "She said as much when she called the house earlier."

"She—she called?" Natalie asked, confused.

"Yeah. She said you and Michael Jones had left the meeting and she realized she didn't even have your cell number." Deanna paused. "The same Michael Jones we saw outside of the hat shop yesterday?"

Natalie swallowed. "One and the same."

"He was trying to talk to you yesterday, wasn't he?" Deanna asked.

Natalie shifted in her seat. "He said hello."

Deanna narrowed her eyes. "I got the sense it was more than that."

"Like what?"

"I dunno. Like maybe he was interested. But you wouldn't give him the time of day. Now you're actually working with him?"

"It wasn't that I didn't want to give him the time of day," Natalie stressed, not quite meeting Deanna's gaze. "It was that I was trying to get away from that pest of a reporter."

"Michael Jones," Callie chimed. "He's hot."

"I guess," Natalie said, feeling her body temperature rise.

"You *guess?* Come on, sis. You'd have to be blind not to see how gorgeous he is."

"Sure, he's cute."

"He's a lot more than cute," Deanna protested. "And I didn't even get an up-close view of him. Lucky you—getting the chance to work with him."

Natalie forced a smile. Then she faced Callie. "I'm surprised you know who Michael Jones is. I didn't figure you for a football fan."

"I love football," Callie said. "Nigel used to play in school, remember? And Kwame's a fan. We watch some NFL games together."

"Oh." Natalie paused briefly. "What do you know about Michael Jones?"

"He's one of the star players," Callie told her. "Wide receiver. He's a fan favorite."

"The ladies love him," Deanna added. "That's what I hear."

No doubt, Natalie thought. "And I'm sure he loves them."

"He's never been married," Deanna said. "Yes, I keep up with all the gossip," she added with a sheepish smile. "Not that I hear everything, but I saw a program where he was touted as one of America's most eligible bachelors. So far, he's not settling down."

"Why choose one when you can have many?" Natalie quipped.

Deanna frowned. "Okay, let's change the subject. We don't want to stray into Vance territory."

"Yes, let's," Natalie agreed. "What were you thinking of doing for July Fourth? Because I was thinking that might be a great time to have a cookout-slash-engagement party."

"Oh, yes!" Deanna agreed. "Great idea."

"Which won't leave us much time to plan," Natalie went on, "but we only need to invite extended family. How's Nigel with the grill?"

"It might be a moot point," Callie said. "If Nigel heads to California next week, then he'll likely be away on the Fourth."

"Oh." Natalie frowned. "Right." And then her iPhone rang. It was on her lap. She quickly lifted it and accessed the text message.

I see you like to make a brother sweat! Let me know when you're free to discuss business again.
I have a few ideas.
—Mike

Natalie felt a jolt. Michael had her number? Of course—Penelope must have given it to him.

"Everything okay?" Callie asked, sounding concerned.

"Oh." Natalie had to make a better effort at masking her emotions. "Nothing. Well, just something about the charity. When to schedule the next meeting. I'll deal with it later."

Chapter 8

Later turned out to be in three days, when Natalie couldn't realistically ignore Michael's calls and texts any longer.

He had called a couple of times and left voice mail messages when Natalie had not picked up. He had also periodically sent text messages, asking that she get back to him in order to schedule the next meeting. Natalie had contacted him only after the second day, telling him that she would be in touch soon.

She knew she wasn't being professional, but she wanted to avoid leading Michael on. Not responding to him for two full days was certain to get the message through to him that their interaction was to be strictly business.

Now, as she headed toward A Taste of Soul, she hoped that Michael was going to be able to do the same.

It was a bit before four-thirty, which meant she was entering the restaurant just in time for the scheduled time of their meeting. Penelope wasn't going to be joining them, which was why Natalie had agreed to meeting at the restaurant again. It would just be her and Michael going over their preliminary plans—something she wanted to do in a public place.

She entered the restaurant, which appeared to be at about a third of capacity. Already, it was lively with chatter. Natalie didn't doubt that the place would fill up in the next couple of hours.

Looking around, she didn't immediately see Michael and wondered where he was. Less than a minute later, he appeared walking from the kitchen entrance. And dear God, just one look at him…

He was wearing a fitted black T-shirt, which was tucked into blue jeans that didn't do a bit to hide just how seriously fine his lower body was.

All of him was fine. There wasn't one area in which he was lacking.

Lifting her gaze, her eyes connected with Michael's. His lips curled in a smile.

Natalie's heart accelerated. Had he noticed that she'd been checking him out?

Perhaps. But she couldn't help herself. Michael wasn't just attractive. He had a warm quality that she was certain drew people to him.

"Ah, you're here," he said cheerfully as he approached her, his voice deep and sexy.

"Hello."

"Good to see you," he added.

Nodding, Natalie looked up at him awkwardly, unsure if she should shake his hand, just stand there, or—

Michael took the choice away from her, opening his arms and giving her a hug. "I'm a hugger," he said. "Hope you don't mind."

"Sure," Natalie said, keeping her voice level. Though her

body undeniably heated as his muscular arms enveloped her, she kept her back ramrod-straight, not hugging him back.

How was it that his touch felt so good, when she should feel nothing at all?

"Dang, you smell good," he went on.

Did she? She had dabbed some natural coconut oil on her neck and pulse points. It was a scent people always complimented her on. Nonetheless, having Michael tell her that she smelled good was not what she wanted, and Natalie quickly backed out of his arms. This meeting was getting off to an unprofessional start.

Michael's eyes swept over her, slowly, clearly taking in everything about her. It was the kind of look that left her feeling flushed. Because the way his eyebrows rose and his smile spread said that he thought she had gotten all dolled up for him.

Had she? Not specifically. Natalie liked to dress up, had a closet filled with beautiful clothes and shoes. Of course she would wear something flattering when meeting with Michael again. Her low-cut blouse, miniskirt and jeweled sandals were about her desire to look good all the time, rather than to impress some playboy.

"And you certainly look good."

"Thank you," Natalie said. Then, "Shall we get started?"

"Of course."

Michael turned first, leading the way. Like she had the last time she was here, Natalie found herself shamelessly checking out his form.

Once again she felt flushed, and had to wonder why she would even check Michael out. Hadn't she learned her lesson with Vance?

Okay, so maybe she missed the idea of having a man in her life. Especially now, when Vance was flaunting his relationship with Olivia all over the place. Clearly there had to be a reason why she was physically attracted to a man like Michael Jones, when her brain knew full well that getting involved with someone like him would only send her down a path of disaster.

It's okay to look, she told herself as he stopped at the booth where they'd been the last time.

"Something to drink?" he asked as he faced her.

"No, thanks. I'm fine." She slipped into the booth. "Let us get down to business, then?"

"Definitely."

Natalie couldn't help thinking that his response had a double connotation as he sat across from her. It was the way he held her gaze so steadfastly, as though trying to make her melt.

She cleared her throat. "I trust you were able to get through to all the people on your list?"

"All but three," Michael said. He opened the folder he had already placed on the table. "A couple of the musical acts declined. One group is going to be out of town on tour. One artist asked for a hefty fee. I explained this was for charity, but she wouldn't budge. Which is okay, because I think we'll have that area covered. I got yeses from a good number of the people I called, though. A local painter, for example, is willing to donate an entire collection of her work for the auction."

"That's wonderful," Natalie said.

"Yep. Things are moving forward."

"I'm so pleased."

She smiled at him, a genuine, impromptu smile, and warmth flowed through Michael's chest as if he'd had a shot of brandy. He allowed himself a moment to stare at her, take in the sight of her as a relaxed person. Natalie was a beautiful woman, but when she smiled, she was extraordinary.

Suddenly, her eyes widened and then her lips went flat.

She had realized that he was taking a moment to observe her, and it was back to business.

She cleared her throat again. "I, too, got through to most of the people on my list. Pastor Browne is more than happy to join us and say the grace. A suspense author is going to donate his five novels—autographed, of course—to the auction. There are a lot of duplicates in terms of the type of performers on the list, so one of the things I'd like to talk to Penelope about is how she'd like us to narrow down the list. Her ideal wish list of whom she'd like to participate."

"Right."

"I don't think we want the time line to go beyond five hours, and that includes a cocktail hour while people peruse the items available for the silent auction." Natalie shifted herself in the booth, causing the frilly edges of her blouse to flutter. Michael couldn't help it—his eyes were drawn to where the delicate fabric had shifted.

Her cleavage.

As far as breasts went, Natalie's were pretty much perfect. Bountiful and firm. The kind that gave her a true hourglass figure.

She was a ten out of ten.

No, make that a fifteen.

He knew she was still speaking, and yet he was no longer hearing what she was saying. He was wondering how Vance could have let someone like her walk out of his life.

And to so publicly dump her? Michael wasn't the type to keep up with gossip, but he usually paid attention to the bigger stories that had to do with fellow athletes.

And all he could think right now, as he was mesmerized by Natalie's beauty, was that Vance had been a total idiot.

It wasn't just because Natalie was extraordinarily beautiful—though that was certainly a compelling reason—but also because she was a woman of principle. He'd realized that in the short time he had known her. He had also done his research, looking up stories about her on the internet, where his view of her had only been confirmed. Natalie was dedicated to giving back to the community and volunteered endlessly.

That was enough to intrigue Michael. He had dated women who were so enamored with his status as a football player and how his checkbook could enhance their lives that giving back was the last thing on their minds. Michael appreciated that Natalie wasn't just a pretty face, but a woman of substance.

She was exactly the kind of woman he was interested in getting to know better. He wanted to take her out, spend time with her on a personal level and see where things might lead.

But Natalie had already made it clear she wasn't interested in getting to know him beyond a business relationship. Typically, Michael would let that be and accept that there was no further reason to even go there. There was always another woman willing to spend time with him.

At least that had been his motto years ago, when one flaky woman after another had gotten involved with him because of what he did, not who he was. Even the one girlfriend he'd had for over a year had bailed when the going had gotten tough after his mother had been in that life-altering car accident.

In large part because of that accident, Michael was a changed man. When someone you loved was nearly taken from you, it became pretty clear what mattered in life. Though the media still speculated as to why he wasn't married and figured him a playboy unable to be tamed, he wasn't that man. Sure, he'd dated his share of women, but he had gotten to a point in his life where he didn't want to date someone just to have any warm body next to him in bed.

And he was fascinated by Natalie. Enough that he knew he was going to throw his playbook out the window. He wasn't going to take her rejection in stride and keep moving, as he typically would. Not when he was certain her attitude had everything to do with her breakup with Vance. Men like Vance gave all athletes a bad name, a stereotype Michael had been fighting ever since he'd signed his first pro contract. So he couldn't blame her for wanting to shut him down. But he'd be damned if he let Vance's behavior get in the way of him getting to know Natalie better.

"At least, that's my opinion," she said.

Man, that voice. So fluttery and sweet. Michael was enjoying watching her speak, even if he had tuned out most of her words.

Natalie paused midsentence and stared at Michael. "What do you think?" she asked.

"I…I think it sounds great," he said, unsure what she was talking about.

"So you think it's great if we offer a trip to Mars for the highest bidder?" she said doubtfully, twisting her mouth.

"Huh? What? *Ohhh.*" Michael finally got it. "Sorry. I missed your last comment."

She shook her head. "You're paying no attention to me, are you?"

"Of course I'm paying attention. My mind just drifted."

She stared at him as if she didn't believe what he was saying. And then, with an accusatory glare, she crossed one arm over her breasts, effectively limiting his view of her cleavage.

As well she should. What had gotten into him? "Please," he began, "repeat your point."

"I was saying that it's all fine and dandy to have artists and local stores donate items for the auction. But we need something bigger. We both have major celebrity connections. We need to get some of our high-profile friends to donate autographed memorabilia, because those items can fetch a pretty penny."

"I was thinking the same thing."

Natalie looked doubtful. "Really?"

"Seriously. In fact, I already talked to a couple of the guys on my team about donating their personal jerseys, or getting everyone to autograph a football. Maybe even offer a special photo session with a fan and his or her favorite player."

Natalie leaned back in her seat. She was surprised. With the way Michael had been looking at her, she was beginning to think that all he'd been interested in was *her,* as opposed to the event. "I'm impressed."

"Good. I aim to please."

Not wanting to hold his gaze too long, Natalie glanced at her folder. "I'm glad we're on the same page with this, because I think it's a great idea. Items from sports figures and the like are invaluable, and people will definitely pay a greater price for those kind of items that you can't simply buy in a store. It might take some arm-twisting—"

"But I won't take no for an answer," Michael said. "You and me, together, we'll get it done."

Natalie narrowed his eyes. Were his words carefully calculated for her?

She glanced to the left as the hostess led two couples to the booth next to them. The people glanced in their direction, and Natalie saw one of the men's eyes light up with recognition. As he nodded at Michael, the other three people quickly realized who Michael was and began to smile.

"Do your thing," Natalie told him, expecting him to get up and bask in the glow of fan adoration.

Instead, she witnessed Michael act in a completely down-to-earth manner. He rose from the booth, greeted the folks at the table with handshakes all around, then asked how they were doing and if they had ever been to the restaurant before.

Natalie couldn't hear everything he said, but within moments, everyone at the table was laughing. Michael was amiable, not at all the stuck-up athlete. Natalie felt bad for having misjudged him.

Turning back to her, he winked, then said, "I'll be back in a minute."

Natalie busied herself looking at the files, but she was really trying her best not to wonder what the wink meant. Not to wonder why a mere look from Michael made her hot and bothered.

A couple of minutes later, Michael returned holding a tray of drinks. The six tumblers looked exactly the same—filled with a pale green liquid and lots of ice, and garnished with a lime wedge.

Michael passed each of the people at the table a drink, then placed the tray on their table. He put a tumbler in front of Natalie, then took a seat before lifting the last drink off of the tray.

"I didn't need a drink," Natalie told him.

"Sure, but as I was giving out some complimentary cocktails, I couldn't ignore you. Besides, it's my specialty. Made it myself. Lime juice, with vodka and a splash of rum. I call it Touchdown."

"Ah," Natalie said. "Nice. Well, in that case…"

Michael lifted his glass. "A toast."

"Okay." Natalie lifted her glass, as well.

"To the fundraiser," Michael said. "And to new friendships."

"Cheers." Natalie clinked her glass against Michael's, then sipped the drink. "Oh. This is good."

"Thank you."

She placed the glass back on the table and returned her attention to the folder. "Now, back to the fundraiser."

"I have an idea," Michael said before she could go on.

"Oh?" Natalie asked.

"In addition to memorabilia from celebrities, how about auctioning off a dinner with me?"

Natalie smirked. "A dinner with you?"

"Women love that sort of thing," Michael said. "Firefighters have done it with huge success. I'm still single, allegedly one of Cleveland's most eligible bachelors." He flashed that charming smile at her. "I bet someone will pay a high price for a night out with me."

Natalie swallowed. There it was. The ego. "I see that you have a high opinion of yourself."

"Does that mean you don't think I'm a good catch?"

There was a playful look on his face, one mixed with confidence. He knew very well that he was a good catch, and wanted to hear her say otherwise.

"You're a successful athlete. For many, that makes you a good catch."

"But not for you," Michael challenged.

"How does this have anything to do with me?" Natalie asked. "You know what, forget that I asked. I've got to run, anyway."

"You mean run away."

Natalie got to her feet. "Leaving." She gathered her belongings. "We've concluded our business, and we'll talk in a few days."

She heard Michael chortle as she pivoted on her heel, but she didn't look back at him. There was no point engaging him in any way.

Instead, she took long, confident strides toward the restaurant's exit, hoping that Michael didn't get up and follow her.

Chapter 9

Natalie pushed through the restaurant's front door, throwing a quick glance over her shoulder.

No Michael.

But by the time she got to her car, she heard the swish of a door opening. Turning toward the restaurant, she saw him.

A big part of her wanted to quickly rush into her car. But, remembering Michael's words before—that she was running away—she stopped.

"The more you run, the more I want to chase you," he said without preamble.

Something about the comment excited her at her very core. For a brief moment, she even thought she should be flattered by his attention.

But then she steeled her jaw and mustered a dispassionate expression. Men like Michael were used to getting everything they wanted. Women tripped over themselves to get to someone like him. They sold out their friends, stabbed others in the back. All to get what they wanted—a ring on their finger from that famous athlete.

"Always in the mood to score, I see," she retorted.

"To score?"

"To win. Whatever. You play a competitive sport for a living. I guess it's just part of your personality."

"A personality you know because—"

"Because I've been there, done that," Natalie supplied.

Michael's eyes twinkled. He was finding this amusing. Or maybe he was just finding her to be a challenge. "With Vance," he stated.

"Yes." Natalie swallowed. "With Vance. I've heard all the lines a man in your position can give a woman, and I'm not keen on repeating the mistakes of my past." Natalie exhaled sharply. "Now, if you'll excuse—"

"No. I won't."

In a flash, Michael closed the distance between them and slipped his arms around her waist. She gasped as he pulled her body against the strong wall of his chest.

Barely breathing, Natalie looked up at him, saw the desire pooling in his eyes. Her body temperature began to rise.

Despite herself, she was attracted to him. She didn't want to be, but she was.

"I don't want to hear that because Vance broke your heart, you're taking it out on all men."

"Not all men," Natalie said on a shuddering breath. "Only athletes."

"Not all athletes are the same."

In his arms, feeling the undeniable heat emanating from his body to hers, Natalie wanted to believe that. Wanted to, but she was all too aware that having believed in fairy tales in the past had only lead to heartbreak for her. She knew better.

"I've heard of your reputation," Natalie said. "Quite the ladies' man."

Michael shrugged, unapologetic. "People change."

Now Natalie laughed and found the strength to pull herself out of his arms. "A leopard can't change its spots."

"Maybe not, but a person can grow up." He shrugged again, those wide shoulders looking so delectable beneath his shirt. "What if I told you that I just never met someone I was truly interested in…until now?"

Natalie took a step backward. She did not want to hear what he was saying. She didn't even want to entertain it.

"What exactly are you so afraid of?" Michael asked her. "Are you afraid that I'm going to hurt you, like Vance did? Or are you afraid that you're going to like it if I touch you?"

He took a step forward. Instinctively, Natalie moved backward. But he matched her movements, stepping toward her again. Natalie kept going, until her body came to rest against her rental car. Suddenly, she was trapped with nowhere to go.

Michael made sure of that fact, because he extended both of his arms on either side of her and placed his palms against the car.

Natalie's heart began to pound furiously. She glanced around, saw people walking on the street and knew what they must be thinking. That she and Michael were an item.

"Well?" Michael asked.

Natalie stared at him with what she hoped was an unwavering gaze. She was angry with herself—angry that she was having any reaction to this man.

"Obviously I'm not afraid that I might like it," she quipped. "It's that I know exactly the type of man you are."

"And you know that because you've given me a chance? Or because you're lumping all athletes into one box? Just because Vance screwed you over."

Natalie had to look away. She had to look away because she knew that Michael was right. She knew that he was right and worse than that, she knew that she was fighting a fierce attraction to him. An attraction that made zero sense to her.

"Or are you really afraid that if I kiss you, you'll no longer be able to deny what you feel?"

Natalie guffawed. But she didn't look at him again. She couldn't. She knew that he would see into her soul exactly what she was feeling.

He relaxed one of his arms and placed his finger beneath her chin, forcing her face upward. "Hmm?"

"That is the most ridiculous—"

"Is it?"

He held her gaze for several beats, the look a challenge in itself. One that said, "Bet you can't look away."

And darn it, she couldn't.

His finger delicately moved from her chin along the base of her jaw, causing Natalie to suck in a sharp breath. And then, before she knew what was happening, Michael lowered his mouth onto hers.

It wasn't yet the Fourth of July, but Natalie was undeniably feeling sparks. Seeing them explode behind her closed eyelids. The touch of his mouth against hers…had anything ever felt this good?

Why did she feel such a rush of unstoppable, insane attraction for this man?

Michael's mouth parted against hers. His full, sexy lips felt incredible. And then he suckled her bottom lip, and she felt dizzy from the desire of the feelings his kiss was awakening in her.

Natalie actually moaned in disappointment when he pulled back, leaving her stunned and speechless. Like someone who had been unexpectedly struck by a flying piece of debris, Natalie stared at him in awe, almost unable to comprehend what had just happened.

His lips curling in the slightest of smiles, he said, "Well?"

He was enjoying this! Somehow, from somewhere within her, Natalie found the strength to become enraged. She needed to feel enraged—anything other than the lust that was coursing through her body. "Is that what you do?" she asked, lurching to the right to get away from him. "Run around kissing every woman you meet?"

"You're not every woman."

"Hoping to prove that you're some sort of super stud?"

Michael laughed. "Are you serious? Super stud?"

"I should slap you for that," Natalie told him.

"Slap me?" Michael's eyebrows shot up. "Are you sure you want to slap me? Wouldn't you rather just kiss me again?"

Natalie's eyes bulged to the point where she thought they would pop out of her head. There was no talking to this man. He had a one-track mind. And clearly, he had a lot of experience when it came to women. Because the way he had kissed her had so effectively made her blood start to boil with desire.

But she wasn't going to be one of those women who let her desire overpower her sense of reason. No way, no how. Not with some sexy athlete who had likely bed countless women.

"If you can't keep this about business, then let me know right now. I'll call Penelope and tell her that I need to work with someone else."

"If you feel so strongly, you can resign from the project. I'm sure Penelope can find someone else to take your place. Someone as skilled as you."

"That's *exactly* what I should do."

"Then do it," Michael told her.

He was calling her bluff, and she knew it. She wasn't about to abandon her responsibility to the fundraiser.

"Because if you're so unattracted to me," Michael went on, "there's no reason we can't get past this. If my kiss inspired nothing in you, then hey, I'm not about to waste my time."

"It inspired nothing," Natalie told him, but she couldn't look at him.

"All right, then," Michael said and shrugged. "If that's the case, then that's the case."

That was it? He wasn't going to fight her on it anymore? Why did that thought cause her heart to deflate?

Something weird was happening to her. Something she didn't understand. All she knew was that right now she needed to get away from Michael. Get away from him before she completely lost her mind.

"We'll talk." And then she turned, fumbled with her keys and, after several seconds, succeeded in opening her car door. And then she slipped into the safety of her car, revved the engine and pulled off into traffic.

But no matter how much space she put between her and Michael, she couldn't outrun the memory of his lips on hers.

We'll talk.

Fat chance of that, Michael thought as he watched Natalie's car drive away. He was going to do a lot more than talk to the beautiful Natalie Hart, he knew that much without doubt.

Even though her car had already disappeared, he remained standing on the street, a smile dancing on his face as he looked in the direction of where she had driven.

He had wanted to ask her to stick around at the restaurant tonight, enjoy the live music and festive atmosphere of a Friday evening. Tonight, a popular band with a washboard player would be performing as they did every Friday night. They were a crowd favorite, and Natalie would have enjoyed it.

Michael pursed his lips. Clearly, he had come on too strong.

It was just that he found something absolutely irresistible about Natalie. He was enjoying flirting with her. It was something he hadn't been inspired to do in a long time.

And for all Natalie's talk about not being interested in him, she had melted in his arms when he'd kissed her. He'd felt her lose herself in the kiss, brief as it had been. And his own body had roared to life with scorching heat. The difference between he and Natalie was that he was willing to explore the attraction between them. She claimed she wasn't.

But Michael had never seen a woman quite so flustered around him. Yes, he was used to women throwing themselves at him, offering their panties and hotel room keys. Natalie wasn't doing any of that, but she may as well have been scribbling his name in a notebook with little hearts beside it, that's how certain he was that she was attracted to him.

Every time he looked at her, he felt sparks—the kind of sparks he knew were mutual. Every time his skin brushed hers he could feel an electrical current pass between both of their bodies.

He was intrigued by her. She simply wasn't like any other woman he had ever met.

No way was he going to let her walk out of his life before he'd even had the chance to get to know her better.

Slowly, Michael turned and headed back into the restaurant. Thus far, he had been making his interest in her clear. Now was the time to pull back. Let her miss him a little.

Absence made the heart grow fonder, after all.

And with his football obligations over the next few days, he would be too busy to meet with her. So he'd give her some breathing room, see how she reacted to him after a little time apart.

See if their chemistry would be just as strong as it was now.

Chapter 10

Two whole days and no word from Michael? Not a phone call, not a text?

Natalie actually felt antsy, wondering what was up with him. How could he so easily cut off communication with her after their conversation on the street?

After that kiss…

And good God, what a kiss! She had replayed the memory of his mouth coming down onto hers over and over again.

That kiss had been out of this world, and as much as Natalie had pushed him away, she had felt the glimmer of possibility as she'd driven away.

What if he really does like me?

Only to hear nada from him. After she had lain awake in bed a second night doing nothing but thinking of the feel of his lips on hers, she realized that she had played right into his hands. Stroked his ego by even having a reaction to him.

In fact, maybe it was her own psyche getting to her. The

fact that she was so adamantly telling him that she wasn't interested in him was actually causing her to feel exactly the opposite.

She recalled their parting words on the street.

If you can't keep this about business, then let me know right now. I'll call Penelope and tell her that I need to work with someone else.

Was that why she had heard nothing from him for two solid days? Had he decided to withdraw from working on the fundraiser because of what she'd said?

Natalie actually hoped not. It was too late for either of them to pull out. Promotional material naming the hosts and lead performers had already been sent to the printer. Withdrawing from the fundraiser would be a huge mess.

So she left him a message on Sunday evening when she hadn't heard from him, which he didn't respond to. On Monday afternoon, fearing the worst, she sent him a text message asking him where he was and why she hadn't heard from him.

His reply had been simple. Out of town. Touch base Tuesday evening.

Well, he'd certainly done an about-face, hadn't he? From the calls and texts daily to hardly any communication at all?

Which, by Tuesday, Natalie was really missing—because she truly could have used a distraction after the latest news hitting the media. Vance was going out with Olivia everywhere, and reporters were now speculating that she had a baby bump.

"Don't worry about that fool," her uncle said after they'd eaten lunch. He, Natalie and Deanna had been sitting on the patio in the backyard, enjoying the comfort of a warm day with an overcast sky. Deanna, however, had just gone back into the house to answer the front door.

"I'm trying," Natalie said, wishing she didn't feel so glum.

"I guess I just feel like a fool. How could I have ever married him?"

"He's the one who looks a fool," Uncle Dave said. "Carrying on with such distaste in public." He harrumphed. "Your auntie Jean never did like him."

Natalie made a face as she looked at her uncle. "She didn't?"

"Nope. Said he seemed superficial and into himself. She feared he would do you wrong."

"She never said anything."

"Wasn't her place." Uncle Dave shook his head. "Lord, I miss her."

Reaching across the table, Natalie squeezed his hand, her eyes misting. "I know. So do I."

"She'd be so happy, seeing you and your sisters getting along."

"She *can* see us," Natalie said. "I have to believe that."

Deanna appeared at the patio door. "Hey, Nat. Come in here for a minute."

"Sure." Natalie made her way into the house. She narrowed her eyes when she saw an enormous bouquet of red roses on the kitchen table.

"They're for you," Deanna said, smiling brightly.

"You're kidding me," Natalie said. "But from whom?"

Certainly not Vance.

Michael?

"You mean Michael Jones?" Deanna said, her eyes growing wide.

Natalie's heart lurched when she realized that she had uttered his name aloud. "Um...I don't think so. Why would he send me roses?"

"I can think of one reason," Deanna replied.

Natalie could only imagine what was going on. Michael hadn't been in touch with her because he had been in some willing woman's bed. Now, trying to get back into her good graces before they would have to meet again, he was sending her roses. It was exactly what Vance would have done.

"Send them back," Natalie said.

"You can't send them back," Deanna told her. "The delivery guy's gone."

"Then put them on the front step. Give them to a neighbor. I don't care."

"Does that mean you don't want to see the card?" Deanna dangled it in front of her face.

Natalie didn't want to see the card. Okay, maybe she did. She had already seen the spectacular roses. What harm would it be to see the card and learn what Michael had to say?

Natalie extended her hand. "Okay. Give it to me."

Deanna handed her the card. Once she had the envelope open, Natalie silently began to read.

"Don't keep me in suspense!" Deanna said. "I want to know who sent you this beautiful bouquet." Leaning forward, she sniffed the roses. "If it's really Michael Jones..."

Natalie read aloud. "Don't let the mistakes of other men affect how you live the rest of your life. You're beautiful and I want to get to know you better. Michael."

Deanna snatched the card from Natalie's hand, squealing with delight as she did. "You are kidding me!"

"I don't know why you sound so excited about this," Natalie began. "He's Michael Jones, superstar athlete. Not some janitor working at a high school. Sending a gazillion roses like this is no big deal for him. Men like Michael have deep pockets that can impress women. It doesn't mean anything."

"Michael Jones is fine." Deanna fanned herself with the card. "Seriously, just because he's a football player doesn't mean—"

"Yes, it does. *Player* is the key word." And who knew what he'd been up to over the past few days. He'd gone from practically stalking her to dropping off the face of the planet. "Don't forget, I saw it. All the time."

"I'm just saying, you shouldn't judge everyone the same," Deanna told her. "What harm is there in getting to know him? After all, aren't you working with him? Wait—did I say the brother is *fine?*"

That was exactly the problem. The fact that he was as fine as he was. Natalie was attracted to him on a physical level. Had even felt flattered by his attention.

Attention that he had likely been lavishing on someone else since she had last heard from him.

Oh, no. She did *not* want to be made a fool of again. Michael could send all the roses he wanted to. She wasn't about to put her heart on the line for him.

Later that night, just after ten, Natalie's phone rang. She was just combing through her damp hair after having showered, and quickly placed her brush down on the dresser in front of the mirror and went to her night table to pick up the phone.

Michael's name appeared on the screen. Seeing it, Natalie's stomach fluttered with nerves. She debated not answering at all, but after three rings she picked up.

"Hello?" she said.

"Hey."

The edges of Natalie's lips fought to smile at the sound of his deep voice, and warmth spread in her chest. Seriously, there was something wrong with her. There had to be.

"You've been scarce," she commented.

"Yeah. Football obligations," Michael explained. "You get the roses?"

"I did. Thank you."

"And judging by your tone, you're suspicious. Let me

guess, you think that I was off being a *player,* and sent the roses to cover my tracks."

There was no point denying the truth. "Something like that."

"Here's the flaw with that thinking. I don't owe you an explanation. In football terms, I'm a free agent. I can do what I want."

Natalie said nothing. She noticed that she felt anxious, and couldn't understand why.

"I sent you the roses because I heard about Vance and Olivia," Michael explained. "I figured you might be feeling down about it, and I wanted to brighten your day."

Natalie's heart soared at Michael's words. Lord, she truly was a fool.

She said the only thing she could. "Thank you." And then, "When I didn't hear from you, I kind of thought maybe you didn't want to work with me on the fundraiser anymore. You know…after that conversation we had on the street."

"You're not going to get rid of me that easily."

Michael knew how to flatter her, that was certain. "Penelope would like to see us on the fifth. I was hoping we could have met again before then. But with tomorrow being the Fourth of July, I guess we can't."

"I've got time in the morning, if that'll work."

"You want to meet in the morning?"

"Why not?"

Natalie supposed she could swing it. In the afternoon, she would be going to Callie and Nigel's place for a cookout. "I have a party to attend in the afternoon. A Fourth of July cookout, but also a celebration of my sister's engagement. But yeah, I can make time in the morning."

"At my restaurant?" Michael asked. "Or somewhere else?"

"I suppose it'll be easy enough for me to meet you there."

"Ten?"

"Sounds good."

"Great." Michael paused. "And maybe you'll extend an invitation to your family's cookout."

When Natalie said nothing, Michael went on. "See you in the morning."

"Sure, see you then."

Chapter 11

The next morning, Michael noticed a definite change in Natalie's demeanor when she entered the restaurant. She seemed visibly relaxed, and even gave him a little smile.

Wow, he thought, checking her out from head to toe. She really was incredible. Her dark denim jeans fit her slim thighs and shapely behind perfectly. She was wearing a simple cotton blouse and flip-flops, a marked change from her sexy business attire.

But she was just as sexy dressed down. And he was certain that without her clothes on, she'd be downright delectable…

That was a sentiment he tried his best to keep to himself. Because if he had scared her off when they'd been in a crowded restaurant, how quickly would she run when it was just the two of them here? The place was closed for business for the holiday.

Besides, he had already made it clear he found her attrac

tive on a sexual level. Now was the time to try and woo her the old-fashioned way. Hence the roses.

And he was on his best behavior, talking business without the flirtation. Even though he was very aware of the fact that they were finally alone together.

As she no doubt was, too.

"All right. Looks like our list is coming together nicely," Natalie said. "Tomorrow, we'll have to talk to Penelope about sending out tax slips to the donors. I'll itemize everything we have here, figure out how much they're worth in terms of tax receipts."

"I'm sure Penelope is going to take care of that," Michael said.

"Probably, but I want to be prepared."

Michael nodded. And then he watched her. Watched her as she pushed a lock of her hair behind her ear. He took in her beauty, savoring it the way one savored fine art.

Her eyes rose quickly, meeting his. And there it was. A definite jolt of attraction between both of them.

Natalie lowered her eyes.

"No," Michael said softly. "Don't."

Slowly, she raised her gaze to his. He just stared, taking a moment to really look at her without her hiding from his gaze.

"How did you know where to send the roses?" she asked after about thirty seconds, seemingly needing to fill the silence with words.

"I asked Penelope."

"They were very nice. Very thoughtful. Thank you again."

"No problem."

Michael watched her do her best to avoid his gaze as she gathered papers and stuffed them into the folder. He even watched as she rose from the table, knowing that she was once again preparing to walk away from him.

She wasn't running, but she was leaving all the same—likely because things had gotten hotter between them.

"All right. Penelope said we could call in the morning, set up a time for later in the day. Will that work for you?"

Saying nothing, Michael rose. Without heels on, she looked even smaller against him.

Delicate. Fragile.

She'd needed someone to protect and honor her, not trample all over her heart.

Her eyes narrowed as she looked at him. "Michael?"

"Yes?"

"Did you hear me?"

"Yes."

Michael was simply standing there, looking at her so intently, as if transfixed. Prickles of heat spread across Natalie's skin.

"I have a question of my own," he said.

And then he reached for her, his fingers skimming her arm. A shuddery breath oozed out of Natalie.

"Did you think about me over the past five days? Did you think about my lips on yours?"

Natalie felt a stab of lust. But she didn't respond.

"I see it in your eyes," he said. "I see how you feel."

Natalie wanted to deny his words, but she could hardly breathe, much less utter a word.

"And yet, I also see your hesitation. Which is really making me question what I should do. By now, another woman—"

"I'm not your average groupie."

"Thank God for that. But still, I don't want to feel like you're always running. Eventually, the lion has to catch its prey."

And, oh, how it might feel wonderful to let him catch her. She swallowed. "Were you really away for football business? Or…"

"Or with some woman?" Michael asked, using the fingers of his other hand to gently caress the skin of her other arm. It was a double assault—one she was powerless to resist.

"Is it really that impossible?" Her voice was husky.

"I've had my share of women, yes," he admitted, his eyes locked on hers. "But none like you."

"So that's what you want," Natalie rasped. "To have something different?"

Now his hands went to hers. He took the folder from her fingers and placed it on the table, then took both of her hands into his. "To have *you*."

What was it about this man that made Natalie want to rip her clothes off and let him take her right here on the table? He was saying all the right things. Keeping eye contact. Making it seem as if she was the only woman in the world.

In *his* world.

And right now, Natalie felt as though she was. As he stared into her eyes, all she wanted was for him to lower his lips to hers and kiss her until every one of her reservations disappeared.

He was a man who knew how to kiss. No doubt he was an extremely skilled lover.

A jolt of heat hit her center. Was she actually thinking about what it would be like to make love to this man?

Oh, yes. Most definitely, she was.

A small smile tugged at the corners of Michael's mouth, and he then began to lower his face to hers. As he did, he pulled her hands to urge her closer. Natalie was like an animal trapped by the headlights of a car—unable to move, unable to look away.

And finally, his mouth came down on hers. Oh, those lips… It wasn't a full-out tongue-in-your-mouth assault, which she couldn't have resisted if her life had depended on it. But in a way, it was the kind of kiss that was far more dangerous.

The slow, sweet kiss.

His lips met hers in the most delicate of ways, the kind that made it clear Michael was a man capable of great intimacy. A soft peck here, another soft peck there. And then he took her bottom lip between his and gently suckled.

Natalie couldn't think. Only feel. And the feeling was amazing. The soft movements of his mouth and tongue elicited the sweetest sensations.

It was the kind of kiss that made a woman light-headed.

And when she moaned, Michael finally groaned into her mouth, pulled his hands from hers and framed her face. The kiss deepened then, his tongue insistently moving into her mouth. Natalie parted her lips, allowing him access, and wondering why she had never in her life felt this kind of explosive sensation at kissing any other man.

Not even Vance.

And God help her, Michael's hands began to move from her face to her neck, and her body was beginning to overheat.

"Michael…" Her chest heaved with each heavy breath. "I…"

He kissed her cheek. "I know. I have to take my time with you. I just wanted to give you a kiss that wouldn't make you want to slap me."

Slap him? What was he talking about? And then she remembered. Goodness, she could hardly think straight.

"You don't want to slap me, do you?"

Not hardly! What she wanted to do was the furthest thing from slapping him. Slowly she shook her head. "No."

"Good." Michael grinned. "All right. I know you want to get going, so I won't keep you."

So after kissing her senseless, he was practically pushing her out the door?

Maybe it was for the best, because if she stayed here, God only knew what they would end up doing.

She gathered her file folder once more. "Tomorrow, then."

She took about five steps away from him when she stopped and turned back. She couldn't believe she was going to do what she was about to do.

"Um, you mentioned somewhat in jest that maybe you could get an invite to my family's Fourth of July cookout. Now, I'm sure you have other plans, but on the off chance that you don't, consider yourself invited."

Michael raised an eyebrow as he looked at her. "Really?"

"Sure," she said.

"I do have somewhere to go—"

"I thought so—"

"But," Michael countered, "not until later. In fact, I was planning on having a quiet Fourth of July. So I'm happy to accept your offer. Just tell me where to go and when."

A tingling sensation spread across the nape of Natalie's neck. Had she really just invited Michael to her family's cookout? It was as if someone else had taken over her body and mind.

It was that kiss. It had her under some sort of spell.

"It's going to be at my sister and her fiancé's place. Anytime after three should be good. That's when the steaks and hot dogs and chicken will be on the grill." She then wrote down the address on a piece of paper from the fundraiser folder she carried and handed it to Michael.

"I'll be there," Michael told her, taking the paper from her hand. He paused, held her gaze. "Should I bring anything?"

"Just yourself," she told him.

Michael brought more than himself. Though his appearance was certainly enough. He came with a couple cases of beer, a case of wine and a tray of desserts. Far more than he needed to.

But it was clear from the excited reaction of all of the people in attendance that his presence alone was akin to them winning a Mega Millions jackpot.

Uncle Dave lit up at the sight of him, which did Natalie's heart good, since she knew how much her uncle was missing Auntie Jean. After introducing Michael to the people in their immediate path, Natalie led him straight to her uncle.

"Uncle Dave, this is Michael—"

"I know who he is," Uncle Dave said, beaming as he reached for Michael's outstretched hand. He gave it a hearty shake. "Most passes caught last three seasons. Mr. Michael Jones, in the flesh. It's a pleasure."

"The pleasure's all mine, sir."

"You call me Dave, you hear?"

Michael nodded. "Okay. Want a beer? Or wine? I brought some from my restaurant."

"A beer from my favorite wide receiver. I must be dreaming."

"I figured you for a beer guy," Michael said. "Heineken?"

Uncle Dave chortled. "How can I refuse?"

"I'll be back in a sec," Michael said.

Once he'd walked away, Uncle Dave squeezed Natalie's hand. "You didn't tell me you and Michael were involved."

"Working together," Natalie clarified. "We're working together on a charity fundraiser. I told him about the cookout, he said he wanted to come by. So here he is."

"Hmm," Uncle Dave said, but he regarded her with curiosity, as if assessing for himself if something was brewing between them.

It didn't get better when Michael met her sisters. Deanna greeted him with a wide smile, as if he were family, then she offered him a hug. But as her arms were wrapped around the wide receiver, she made a face at Natalie that screamed, *My God, he's gorgeous! How lucky are you?*

It turned out that Callie was truly a fan, because she

gushed when she met Michael, and quoted some of his football stats which Natalie didn't understand. Natalie hadn't realized that her sister was that into football. Of course, they hadn't spoken in ten years, so it wasn't surprising that there were things about her she didn't know.

Michael made his rounds, clearly the center of attention. It struck Natalie then that all of the extended family was Uncle Dave's. His nephews and nieces, his two brothers. Auntie Jean had been her mother's only family, but Natalie hadn't questioned until now—at least not in a serious way—where the rest of their family was.

It seemed as though the kids couldn't wait to get their hands on Michael, because once he'd finished greeting the adults, Kwame and his young cousins swarmed Michael, most of them talking at once. And the next thing Natalie knew, they were rushing him down the deck steps and leading him onto the grass. Kwame held a football under his arm.

Deanna took a seat beside Natalie. "Girl, if that man ain't fine, then no one is. What a great way to get over Vance."

"Excuse me?"

"Do you know his sign?" Deanna went on. "You're a Scorpio, so you'd be good with a—"

"What do you mean by 'great way to get over Vance?'" Natalie interrupted.

Deanna flashed her a lopsided grin. "Come on. You must have considered it. He's *gorgeous*."

"You like him so much, I'll let him know."

Now Deanna looked confused. "No—you don't think I like him like *that*, do you? Of course not. Sis, I'm never going to let a man come between us again."

Realizing how Deanna had misconstrued her words, Natalie squeezed her arm and shook her head. "Dee, that's not what I meant. No, definitely not. It's just…"

It's just that she was testy, as her sister's words had hit a nerve. Michael *was* gorgeous. But he was a professional athlete, and they were notorious for being unfaithful. A lesson she had learned the hard way.

Natalie glanced in Michael's direction, saw his magnificent body stretched as his arm extended to throw the football. "He *is* fine. With a capital *F.* But I've only just ended things with Vance."

"Vance is a Sagittarius, right? Sagittarius men are so often cheaters. Find out if Michael is a Taurus. They tend to be faithful."

"You sound totally crazy right now," Natalie said, and giggled.

"I just want to see you happy."

At Deanna's words, Natalie couldn't help glancing in Callie and Nigel's direction. Callie had her arms looped around Nigel's waist as he stood at the grill, turning over the burgers. They looked blissfully in love.

"I appreciate that." Natalie offered her sister a soft smile. "But listen, on a more serious note. We never really questioned where Mom and Auntie Jean's family was. We were told they lived in another state and never questioned it. But seeing Uncle Dave's family surrounding him now...where's our mother's family?"

Deanna frowned. "I don't know. Auntie Jean never said much. Nothing really. I always got the sense that it was just her and our mother, that maybe the rest of the family had died or something."

"What if they didn't? What if they're around somewhere? That could be where our mother is."

"Then we have to talk to Uncle Dave," Deanna said. "Not now, of course, but later. Because if anyone knows anything, he should."

Natalie nodded. Then as she heard the kids squeal, she

looked down onto the grass. Michael was flat on his back, and the kids were piling onto him.

Natalie shot to her feet and headed down the steps. "Not too rough now," she said as she wandered closer to the mass of bodies. "Michael's got a football career to think of."

The kids eased off of him, and Kwame offered him his hand to help him up. Looking at her, Michael said, "I'm all right. We're having fun, right kids?"

They agreed enthusiastically.

Natalie grinned. She liked that Michael was not only down-to-earth, but great with kids.

He walked close to her and said, "But it's nice to know you're concerned about me."

Natalie's lips parted, but she said nothing. If she denied that she was concerned, that would sound wrong. But if she agreed that she was, that could also be misconstrued.

Of course, she had already enjoyed one of the hottest kisses in her life with him only hours earlier. One that had her thinking of the fact that he had to be incredible in the bedroom….

"Okay," Nigel called out above the old-school music playing on the stereo system. "The burgers are ready. Anyone who wants one, get 'em before they're gone."

The kids rushed onto the deck, leaving Michael and Natalie standing on the grass. "You don't want a burger?" Natalie asked him.

"I kind of want something else."

With the way Michael bit down on his bottom lip and made steady eye contact with her, it was clear what he was talking about.

And she could hardly believe it, but she wanted that something else, too. Another scorching kiss that made her forget everyone but Michael existed.

"I'm going to go in the house." She pointed a thumb over

her shoulder. "Get the potato salad, maybe make some more lemonade."

Michael nodded. "You go ahead."

Natalie began to turn, then she stopped. Instead, she held his gaze and said, "I'm glad you came by. Everyone's really excited."

"And you?" Michael challenged. "Are you excited?"

A beat passed, then she offered him a tiny smile and said, "A little."

And just before she turned to head into the house, she saw his eyes widen ever so slightly, registering his surprise at her admission.

About an hour and a half later, everyone began to whistle and clap after Uncle Dave finished getting down to George Clinton and the Parliament Funkadelic.

"Oh, my," Callie said. "I didn't know you could move like that, Uncle Dave."

People were laughing. Everyone was having a good time. Natalie, who was leaning against the deck railing holding a glass of wine, noticed as Michael pushed his chair back from the patio table and stood.

"And on that note," Michael began, "I've got to go."

There was a hum of disappointment, and protests from many.

"I've got somewhere else I need to be," Michael explained. "But I thank you all for having me."

Nigel approached Michael with his hand outstretched. "Any time," Nigel told him. "We hope you come back."

"You fit right in," Callie said. "Just like family." She shot a glance at Natalie.

Natalie felt a spurt of panic. Then her gaze went from Callie's to Deanna's. Deanna was smirking at her, and Natalie was certain that she and Callie had spoken about the idea of Michael being the new man in her life.

But her attention soon turned to Michael, who was making his way over to her. "Walk me out," he said.

Natalie rested her wineglass on the wooden railing. "Sure."

A minute later, they were outside, approaching Michael's car. "So," Natalie began, wondering why her stomach was fluttering, "where are you off to?"

"Not a party." Michael stopped in front of his car. "Gonna visit my mother for a bit."

"Oh." That wasn't what Natalie had expected. And for some reason, sadness washed over her. Michael was going to see his mother, while she had no idea where on the planet hers was.

"Hey," Michael said softly. "What's the matter?"

Natalie shook her head, but she had to dab at the tear that fell from her right eye. "Nothing."

Michael took a step toward her, placing a hand on her upper arm. "You're crying."

"I'm sorry. It's just…you mentioned your mother…"

"And?" Michael prompted when she didn't finish.

"And…well, long story short, my sisters and I don't know where our mother is. We haven't seen her in twenty-three years."

"What?" Michael's eyes registered his shock.

"It's…a long story. One for another time. But I want you to know that I'm really glad you came today. Everyone loved having you here. Especially my uncle. His wife—my auntie Jean—died a couple of months ago, and it's been a really tough time. It's one of the reasons my sister and I are in town. To spend time together as a family and to be here for my uncle. Your presence here today really helped lift his mood, so thank you for that."

Michael gently rubbed his hand up and down Natalie's

arm, offering her comfort. "I'm sorry for your loss," he said. "And for whatever's going on with your mother."

"Thank you."

"You all have gone through a lot recently, and I'm honored you allowed me to spend time with your family." He paused, held her gaze. "I had a great time, too."

Natalie's lips curled in a small smile. "Good. I'm glad." She sighed. "Please, ignore my getting emotional."

"I don't mind it. In fact, if you ever want to talk about your mother or anything else, I'm happy to listen."

He sounded sincere, and Natalie appreciated the offer.

He was still touching her, his hand resting on her shoulder. Then he tucked a strand of her hair behind her ear, and an entirely different emotion came over Natalie now. She felt a tingle of desire.

Staring up at Michael, Natalie said nothing, and neither did he. He just looked at her as if he wanted more.

Natalie waited, surprised to realize that she wanted more, as well. Yet Michael made no move to kiss her.

Instead, he reached into the pocket of his jeans to retrieve his car keys. The BMW beeped as the doors unlocked.

Natalie scrunched her forehead. That was it? Not another hot kiss?

Clearly, Michael had read her mind. Because he nodded in the direction of the house. "We've got an audience."

Natalie whipped her head around. She saw the sheer curtains suddenly close.

"Oh. Of course." No doubt her sisters. Heck, maybe the whole family.

"Like I said, I had a good time. It was nice spending time with your family. And with you."

"Talk to you tomorrow, then," Natalie said.

He winked at her. "Sure thing."

Chapter 12

Perhaps Natalie should have avoided looking Michael up on the internet, but everyone did that these days, so later that evening, as she hadn't been able to stop thinking about him, she did just that.

And the elation she had been feeling earlier dissipated as she checked out a particular blog about cheaters which had come up when she had entered his name in the search engine. While the posters were anonymous, Michael Jones, famed wide receiver, was most certainly not. He was outed as a liar and a cheater and a heartbreaker. The thread had been started by a scorned woman only three months earlier, and she went on and on about how Michael had promised her the world, then dumped her for someone else. Other women—allegedly, since the responders were also anonymous—concurred with the original post, stating that their own experiences with Michael had left them devastated. Their strict warning to anyone reading the blog was to stay away from him.

Natalie read every single entry, her stomach feeling sicker and sicker as she did. Finally, she turned off her laptop and closed it with disgust.

She had begun to let her guard down where Michael was concerned, and had been especially touched by his concern over her mother and the loss of her aunt. He genuinely seemed to care, and that fact had warmed Natalie's heart for the rest of the day.

Until she'd found that website.

Now, with an unlikely sense of disappointment, Natalie was now reerecting a wall around her heart. A part of her knew that she couldn't take the word of anonymous posters on a site like this, but another part reminded her that she herself had wanted to stay away from Michael because of the fact that he was an athlete. An athlete who faced far more sexual temptation than the average man. Men like Michael found it almost impossible to say no.

By the next morning, Natalie was feeling more anxiety than she had in a long time. She didn't want to see Michael again, didn't want him to give her that look that made her feel like the most beautiful woman in the world. In fact, when she saw Penelope's number appear on her phone, Natalie was preparing an excuse as to why she couldn't make it to the meeting today. Until she heard Penelope's words.

"I know this is last minute," Penelope began, "but I have an offer for you and Michael to appear on a noon radio show. *The Josh and Jane Show.* I was hoping for a couple of days from now, but they said that if you can swing it for today it would be great as they have a cancellation. I already spoke to Michael, and he's free."

Natalie swallowed.

"This is a great opportunity to promote the event. Please tell me you're not busy," Penelope said.

No matter how much she wanted to, Natalie knew that she couldn't say no. This *was* a great opportunity.

"I'm available," she said, mustering her best cheerful voice.

"Great." Penelope sounded hugely relieved. "They'll need you to arrive at the studio between eleven-forty-five and noon, which is almost three hours from now."

"I'll be there."

"Wonderful. I'm so glad. And again, I'm sorry about the last minute."

"No problem. That's how it is sometimes. You take advantage of the opportunities when they present themselves."

"You truly are a pro," Penelope said. "Let me give you the address and the name of who you're asking for once you get to the station."

At eleven-fifty-five, Natalie rushed into the radio station. She had been delayed in traffic backed up from an accident en route to the station, and hoped that her arrival wasn't too late.

The fact that she was later than she'd hoped to be had her feeling a little on edge as she entered the lobby. As did the fact that she knew she would run into Michael any second.

She gave her name to the person at the security desk, got a visitor's pass, and within a minute a woman with a headset emerged from a pair of double doors to meet her.

"Natalie Hart?" the woman said.

"Hi. I'm sorry I'm late. I—"

"No problem. We've got time." The short, chubby blonde smiled brightly. "I'm Gloria. Great to meet you."

"Likewise."

"Follow me."

Gloria led her through the double doors she had come from only a minute before, behind which was a bank of elevators. They took the elevator to the fifth floor.

"It's certainly a hot summer," Gloria said.

"Yes, definitely. And I thought Texas was hot."

They exited the elevator. The long corridor was bright white and had photos of people who had to be various personalities on the walls. Nothing glamorous, but so often radio and television stations were not.

They entered another set of doors, and then, *Bam!* Natalie's heart slammed against her rib cage as she laid eyes on Michael.

He looked up from the seat he was occupying and smiled, and as Natalie's pulse began to race, she realized that Michael's smile was some sort of secret weapon. Hadn't one of the posters to the blog said something to that effect? That when Michael smiled at her, she had believed she was the only woman in the room?

Indeed, Natalie hadn't even noticed the two other people in the room until one of them stood. An attractive male only slightly taller than she approached with his hand outstretched.

"Natalie Cooper."

"Hart," Natalie corrected.

"Oops, that's right." The man had a deep voice, a great voice. No wonder he was on the radio. "Sorry about your divorce."

"Thanks."

The woman, who had been sitting next to Michael, laughed at something he said, then finally pulled herself away from him to get up and greet Natalie. And Natalie's heart deflated even more than it had the previous night when she set eyes on the stunning brunette.

That shapely body, those bright blue eyes, the flat-ironed hair… She looked as if she could have been an NFL cheerleader.

Did Michael go for that sort?

"Natalie, I'm Jane. Josh's cohost."

Natalie shook her hand. *Hardly a Plain Jane...* "Nice to meet you," she said.

Michael then got to his feet and approached her. He wrapped his arms around her. "Hey, you."

"Hi," Natalie said tightly, not hugging him back.

She noticed Michael's frown at her frosty reception when he pulled back, but he didn't question it.

"When will the show start?" Natalie asked.

"We've got about ten minutes. We go live after the news."

Natalie nodded. "Okay."

Another man appeared in the room, introduced himself as Craig, the sound engineer. "Natalie, if you'll sit here." He indicated the seat to the far right. "Michael, if you'll sit here." He indicated the seat on the far left.

Then Josh and Jane sat on the two chairs in the middle, clearly their usual spots.

Natalie stared at microphones laid out on the electronic console in front of them as if they were the most interesting things in the world. Then, feeling antisocial, she glanced to her left.

Even with the radio hosts between them, it was disconcerting to be this close to Michael. Any man who could make her take down her guard so quickly was clearly dangerous to her heart.

"Your microphone, Natalie."

Natalie looked up to see Craig standing beside her. He held a small microphone. As he began to attach it to her collar, she felt Michael's eyes burning through her skin. She knew he was staring at her, but pretended that she was oblivious.

"Okay," Craig said, "count from one to ten for me so I can test your microphone."

Natalie complied. Behind a glass wall, a man there gave a thumbs-up after Natalie spoke. Satisfied, Craig moved to

Michael, who had been chatting with Jane, and proceeded to attach the microphone to his collar.

As Craig took care of Michael's microphone, Jane turned to her. "I was sorry to hear about you and Vance breaking up. Ball players…they can be such dicks."

"Yeah," Natalie said softly. "Thanks." She hoped this woman wasn't going to say more on the matter.

When Craig left the room, the male host asked, "Have you done radio before?"

"Yes," Natalie explained. "Pretty much in the same capacity. When I did fundraisers in San Antonio, I did a lot of radio and television to promote the various events."

Harvey smiled at her. "So you're an old pro. Good. And Michael, we've had you on the show once before. Good to have you back."

"Good to be back," Michael said.

"We're just going to ask you about the event you're doing, and we're basically going to have a casual conversation. It's going to be light, and we'll have fun with it. You know how we do the show."

Michael nodded. "Yep."

And then the sound engineers behind the glass wall held up a hand and said, "One minute warning, time to put on your headsets."

Josh, Jane, Natalie and Michael complied, after which they all went quiet. Then the show's theme music came on, and Josh and Jane did their normal on-air banter about local happenings before turning to Natalie and Michael. Natalie had kept her eyes on the hosts as not to have to meet Michael's eyes.

But she knew she wouldn't be able to avoid him once they had to talk.

"We've got two great people here in the studio," Jane

began, "and I have to say, they're also beautiful. I can't help thinking they'd make gorgeous babies."

Josh—in his role as her playful nemesis chastised her. "Sheesh, Jane, is that all you ever think about? Making babies?"

"I'm just saying," Jane went on. And then, "Okay, okay, I'll be serious. Here with us today, we have local celebrity, Cleveland wide receiver Michael Jones, and he's here with Natalie Hart-Cooper. Yes, *that* Natalie Cooper, but we're not here to talk about her ex."

Natalie forced a smile, though she wanted to roll her eyes.

"And you two are part of a really cool fundraiser," Josh said. "Why don't you tell us about it?"

Michael and Natalie exchanged glances, both of them waiting to see who would speak first. Michael gestured toward her, letting her know that she should take the lead.

"First of all, I want to say thank you for having us on the show this afternoon and allowing us to speak about a very special fundraiser," Natalie said. "On August 12, there are going to be huge fundraising efforts in support of Compassion For Families."

"What is Compassion For Families?" Jane asked.

Natalie explained the charity's role and purpose. "As you can imagine, in these tough economic times it's even harder for families to maintain medical insurance. No one should have to choose between paying their mortgage and paying for medical treatment for a critically ill child. Every penny of the money we earn will be going directly to help those in need."

There were questions about the venue, the ticket price and who could attend.

"Anyone can attend," Natalie said. "But tickets are limited, so get yours now. There will be local artists performing—including Deanna Hart, R&B singing sensation, who also happens to be my sister."

"Sounds like it'll be a star-studded event," Josh commented. "Michael, how are you involved with the project?"

"I'm being auctioned off to the highest bidder," Michael said.

"Oooh," Jane said. "Now that sounds interesting."

"For sure. All those women out there who have wanted some one-on-one time with me, this is your chance," Michael said with a smile. "The winner of the bid will get to spend an evening with me."

"I will be there and I'll be bringing lots of cash," Jane said, and chuckled. "Seriously."

"I encourage all women to bring lots of cash," Michael said. "After all, it's going to a good cause."

"Can you say *cat fight?*" Jane asked. "All those women clawing over each other to get close to you?"

Enough already, Natalie thought.

"What about for the men?" Josh asked. "A chance to take out the newly single Natalie Hart?"

"No," Natalie said. "But there will be lots of great items to bid on. So I encourage everyone to come out and support this worthy cause."

There was more banter, more information about the event, and the interview ended with laughter.

"That was excellent," Josh said when a commercial break started. He shook her hand first, then Michael's.

"Yes," Jane concurred. "You guys were awesome."

Craig entered the room and helped take off their microphones, then quickly ushered them out of the studio. Because once the commercial break was over, Josh and Jane were going to continue with their show.

"Gloria will escort you back downstairs," Craig said.

Natalie was silent, not paying attention to the small talk between Michael and Gloria in the elevator. Once they hit the main lobby, she faced Gloria and said, "Thanks again. Have a good day."

She started off quickly as Michael said his goodbye, but she didn't make it far. Because no sooner than she stepped outside onto the sidewalk, she felt Michael's arm on hers.

He spun her around, giving her a look of confusion as their eyes met. "Hold up, hold up. You're just gonna leave me in the dust like that…again?"

"I've got things to do."

Michael made a face. "Something to do with your mother?"

Natalie sighed. "No." She paused. "Something else. Something you wouldn't understand."

"Try me."

She didn't want to do this, engage in any conversation with him and give him a chance to get past her defenses. "Later, okay?"

She began to turn, but once again, Michael's hand was on her arm. "You sure you're all right?"

His tone was sincere, the look in his eyes earnest. "Why wouldn't I be?"

"I don't know. You tell me."

"I'm fine. Just…pressed for time."

"Okay." Michael released her arm. "It's just…I was looking forward to seeing you, spending some time with you. I was thinking I could take you out to dinner. You know, a date."

Natalie's heart began a quick pitter-patter. The less than flattering comments she'd read about him the night before were fading, the only thing mattering right now her attraction for him.

Fight it, she told herself. *Don't let him fool you!*

"I'll let you know," she said.

Michael looked unhappy. But he didn't argue. Instead, he simply said, "All right." And then, "Hey, if you need to talk, I'm here."

As if! The last thing she could do was talk to him about what she'd read on the internet.

What she wanted—needed—was to find a way to put him out of her mind. Immediately.

Chapter 13

For the next several days, Michael blew up Natalie's phone with text messages and calls. With much of the necessary initial planning for the gala fundraising event out of the way, it wasn't critical for them to meet as often anymore. Natalie had certain questions and concerns that she had been able to speak directly to Penelope about.

Which had allowed her to avoid Michael.

She hadn't answered his phone calls, but she had responded to some of his text messages—the ones where he'd asked how she was doing—with one word answers like "fine" and "okay." She had ignored his many requests to let him know when a good time to get together for dinner would be.

She knew she must look absolutely wishy-washy to him. One minute melting against him as he kissed her, the next, cold. But after reading those scathing reports about him on the web, her fear about a man like Michael being innately untrustworthy had come roaring back.

She couldn't afford to take a chance with a man like that.

It would be one thing if she weren't attracted to him. Then she could talk to him, meet him for dinner, even hang out without any issue. But she *was* attracted to him, and she could no longer deny that. The truth was, she knew that she had been attracted to him the moment she had first seen him on the street.

He had the exact look, physique and smile that could draw her in. Heck, you would have to be dead not to feel something when a man like Michael Jones looked at you.

The only way to quash what she was feeling for Michael was to cut off all unnecessary communication with him. She knew they would have to talk once the program for the fundraiser was finalized. They would have to determine how they would share their hosting duties—who would say what and when. But Natalie figured they had a couple of weeks before they had to nail that down—two more weeks in which she could get her feelings under control.

She hoped that her minimal responses would have inspired Michael to eventually stop reaching out to her, but it was becoming clearer to her that he would not be deterred. A full week after the radio interview, Natalie was at the mall with her sisters and nephew when Michael called. Three times in a row.

When the phone began to ring for the fourth time, Callie met her gaze from across a rack of blouses and asked, "Aren't you going to answer your phone?"

"I wasn't planning on it."

"You're going to play that hard-to-get act until you really push him away," Deanna said in a warning tone.

Natalie glanced at Kwame, whose eyes were locked on the screen of a Nintendo DS. He wasn't paying attention to their conversation.

"That's pretty much the idea," Natalie said.

"Because of that crap you read on the internet," Deanna said, and rolled her eyes.

Natalie shrugged. "Where's there's smoke, there's fire."

"You want to know the kind of things people said about me on the internet that were *completely* untrue?" Deanna countered. "So much that I don't even look up my name anymore. When you're a public person, people will say a lot of things. Especially jilted gold diggers."

Natalie pursed her lips. Deanna had a point.

"You have no clue what each of those women's motives were," Callie added. "But I wouldn't give an anonymous post any credence."

Natalie's phone rang again. "If you don't get it," Callie went on, "I will."

"Fine." Sighing, Natalie answered the phone and brought it to her ear because Michael would not give up. "Hello?"

"You have to tell me what I did," Michael said without preamble. "Why you're avoiding me."

"I'm not avoiding you," Natalie said in a lowered voice. She took a few steps away from her sisters so that she could have some privacy.

"Right," Michael countered, but his tone was good-natured. "I mean, I'm confused. We were at my restaurant, alone, and shared a passionate kiss. We topped that off with a nice time with your family. The next thing I know, I'm getting a cold reception from you at the radio station. And now you're not getting back to me. So, yeah, I'd call that avoiding someone."

"I've been busy," Natalie said.

"Give me some credit," he replied, his tone doubtful. "If I somehow did something wrong, tell me. Let me make it right."

Fool that she was, Natalie's heart warmed. He really seemed to be trying, when the truth was he could easily be too frustrated to bother with her. And just the sound of his voice brought back the memory of their kiss—one she had tried desperately to forget, because thinking of the kiss only made her want more of him.

"Look…there's just a lot going on. Nigel just left for California and it has to do with my mother."

"Is everything okay?" Michael asked, instantly alarmed.

Instantly Natalie felt bad for using the excuse of her mother as her reason why she didn't have time for Michael. "Truthfully? We're not exactly sure." She sighed softly. "It's not like we're waiting by the phone for word every second…I guess I just feel emotionally spent."

"Maybe an evening with me will help take your mind off of things."

Natalie glanced back at her sisters. They were still perusing the rack of blouses. She stepped out of the store, where it was quieter.

"Just one night," he said. "You may even enjoy yourself," he added, his tone lighthearted.

"Okay," Natalie said. "I'll go out with you."

Michael hesitated, as though unsure he had heard her correctly. "I'm talking a real date here. Candles, wine. The kind of date where we can get to know each other better."

A beat passed, then she said, "Yes. But I don't want you to have any expectations. This is just about two people enjoying each other's company. Not about a relationship or anything like that, because I'm not ready for that."

"If that's the only way I can have you," Michael said, "I'll take it."

The words caused Natalie to flush. She had to admit, she was rejecting Michael more than most women likely did, and he had not yet moved on. Whether it was because they were working together on this fundraiser, or because he was an egomaniac who didn't like to take no for an answer, she didn't know. Or maybe his feelings and intent were truly genuine.

"What do you like to eat?" Michael asked. "Seafood? Steak?"

"Here's what I think. Taking me to some fancy restaurant is easy for you. What I would like is for you to think outside the box. A fancy dinner isn't going to impress me."

"So you want to be impressed?"

Natalie immediately realized her faux pas. "No. I'm not trying to be impressed. I just…I just want a different experience. I want you to make it interesting."

"Fair enough," Michael said. "So what about this Friday night?"

"Sure. Friday's good."

"Great. I'll call you tomorrow to finalize the details."

The call ended, Natalie started back into the store. But then her phone rang again moments later, and Natalie saw Michael's number on the screen once more.

"Yes?" she said, answering quickly.

"Tomorrow," Michael responded. "I want to see you tomorrow."

"Oh."

"Don't say no," Michael said.

Natalie was silent for a moment, then she said, "All right, I won't. Tomorrow."

"Let's plan for five. I'll call back with the details."

"Sounds great."

Natalie ended the call, and this time the phone didn't ring again. She made her way back to her sisters, who were both looking at her expectantly.

"Well?" Deanna asked.

"We're going out tomorrow," Natalie said, her tone matter of fact. "And don't make a big deal about it. It's just a date. Something to do."

"If you say so," Deanna said, then smirked as she looked at Callie.

* * *

The next day, Michael called just before noon. Her stomach fluttering, she answered before the phone rang a third time.

"Hey, Michael."

"Hey, beautiful. How are you?"

A simple compliment, but it left Natalie feeling a measure of excitement she didn't expect. "I'm good. You?"

"I'm great. Looking forward to seeing you later."

"And where are we going?"

"That's still a surprise. Can I pick you up? Around four?"

"Why don't I meet you wherever we're going?"

"Why don't you meet me at my restaurant and we'll go from there?"

"Or I'll follow you from there."

Michael chuckled softly. "Tough cookie. But okay, I can deal with that."

"Four o'clock?"

"That'll be great. And, oh, dress casually."

"Casually?"

"That's my only hint. No fancy outfit, and definitely no heels."

"Hmm."

"See you soon."

At shortly after four, Natalie arrived at the restaurant. She was about to get out of her car when she saw Michael exit the restaurant. So instead, she lowered her passenger side window and called out to him.

"Hey, Michael. You ready?"

Michael came to her open window and rested his elbows on the edge while he peered in at her. "I take it you're not getting out of your car?"

Natalie smiled sweetly. "I figure I'll follow you. That way I'll have my own car if I need to make a fast getaway."

Michael's eyes crinkled as he chuckled. "Nice. But okay. You can follow me." He started to pull back, then stopped. "How hungry are you?"

"I don't understand."

"I was thinking that I'd like to do something other than dinner with you."

Natalie's pulse raced. "Like?"

"Like something else first, then we'll eat. I just want to make sure you're okay not to eat for a bit."

Natalie eyed him suspiciously. "I think I'll survive for a bit."

Easing back, Michael tapped the base of the car window. "All right. Follow me."

Soon, Michael's car was on the move and Natalie was driving behind him. Fifteen minutes later, they were pulling into the parking lot of a roller-skating establishment Natalie had frequented as a kid. She narrowed her eyes, wondering if this was truly the destination.

When Michael parked and exited his car, she saw that it was.

"Roller Palace?" Natalie asked as she got out of her car to meet Michael.

"You weren't expecting this, were you?"

"No. Definitely not."

"Good." Michael paused. "I was hoping you'd look more excited," he added with a twinkle in his eye.

"I haven't been on roller skates in… Well, since I left here."

"Then we're in the same boat. It's been a while for me, too. But I figure the old-school music will have us skating like old pros." Michael placed his hand on the small of her back. "By the way, I'm glad you took my advice and dressed casually."

"I figured we'd be shucking crabs somewhere," Natalie commented wryly.

"The night is young."

As they headed into the rink, Natalie was suddenly nervous. She didn't exactly feel comfortable with the idea of getting on roller skates, because there was a high likelihood that she would make a fool of herself.

Maybe it hadn't been the smartest thing to tell Michael to plan a date that was out of the ordinary. Suddenly, a dinner at a fine-dining restaurant didn't seem so bad, after all.

Stepping into the roller-skating establishment was like taking a step into the past. A Jackson Five tune was blaring through the stereos. Flashing disco balls hung above the large rink. The carpet on the exterior of the rink, though clearly newer, still looked like the same bright red that it had been years ago.

Oh, yeah, this was old-school.

"Where is everybody?" Natalie asked.

Michael grinned at her again, and damn if the man's smile didn't make her insides melt into goo. "I arranged for the place to be empty. It's just me and you and some of the staff."

Natalie swallowed. "Are you serious?"

"Dead serious. I wanted some alone time with you. And if I had to pay the establishment to make it happen, then so be it."

Though Natalie knew that the money was no object for him, she was touched. Because it wasn't simply about the money. It was about the thought. And the truth was, while Vance had had a lot of money, his grand gestures had been typically about buying her fancy trinkets or chocolates on occasion. He didn't put a lot of thought into the types of romantic experiences he could provide for her.

Michael and Natalie headed to the skate rental area, where she got her proper size, a pair of socks, and then put her skates on. Thankfully, she didn't fall flat on her face the moment she was in them. Though she could only take baby steps.

Michael grinned down at her as if he was an old pro. Then

e lost his balance and had to throw out both arms to stop himself from falling.

"I'm okay, I'm okay." He reached for her hand. "Don't worry, I'm here for you."

Natalie gave him a skeptical glance. "Why am I not re-assured?"

"Hey, that was just one unstable moment. Now I'm good."

"All right…"

With her hand in his, Michael walked together with her along the carpeted area until they got to the rink. "If you start to fall, I'll catch you. I promise."

And as much as Natalie wanted to keep her guard up where Michael was concerned, she believed what he said. That if she were to fall flat on her face, he would throw his body onto the floor so that she could land on him.

And she also believed that his words extended beyond their immediate situation, that Michael was the type of man who would catch her when she fell in the real world.

Don't fall too fast, a voice in her head told her.

For a man like Michael, pulling out all the stops could simply be a part of his playbook.

As they headed onto the rink, SWV's "I'm So Into You" from the '90s started to play. Despite Natalie's fear of falling, the music helped get her into the mood to groove. She allowed Michael to guide her slowly around the rink, and soon, her hips were swaying to the music. As were his.

"Like getting on a bike, right?" he said, releasing her hand.

"Not so bad," Natalie concurred. She moved a little faster, feeling the flow. Then she watched as Michael picked up speed. Soon, he was busting out in some goofy old-school dance moves when an Old Dirty Bastard song began to play. She couldn't help giggling. Not only was the man attractive, he was funny.

"Oh, you're laughing at me, are you?" Michael asked.

"Well, you do look a little silly."

"Silly?" Michael paused in front of her. "You think you can do better, show me what you got."

Natalie felt as though a glaring spotlight was suddenly on her. "I didn't say I could do better."

"Come on," Michael urged her. "Give it your best."

Natalie didn't want to, but Michael stood, waiting, and even placed his hands on his hips. She knew she had no choice but to do *something*.

So she did a little hip shake and arm shake as she moved carefully forward. Michael made a cheering sound, which gave her encouragement. Natalie then upped her game, doing a jerking full-bodied shimmy.

"Now that's what I'm talking about." Michael clapped his hands and whistled. But that's when Natalie lost her nerve, and began to giggle.

Michael started to move again, gliding past her with ease. He spun around, skating backward.

"Now you're just showing off," Natalie told him.

He grinned at her. And then he began to shake his hips. Spinning around, he fell onto his butt, and Natalie gasped.

"I'm okay." Michael got to his feet. And he got right back at it, doing a finger in the air hip move reminiscent of John Travolta in *Saturday Night Fever*.

Natalie started to laugh, lost in the moment. She was having a good time.

Suddenly, her problems were forgotten. She knew it was only temporary, but she wasn't worrying about Vance, nor about what would happen in California when Nigel questioned the criminal who had once been involved with her mother.

And she certainly wasn't thinking about the fact that men should be avoided at all costs.

In fact, she was thinking that she wouldn't mind…

No, she was not thinking *that*. Absolutely not. She wasn't

going to go there. She wouldn't go from thoughts about kissing him to thoughts of getting naked.

"You know, I came here the night of my high school prom," Natalie said.

"After your prom, you came here?" Michael asked. "With your date, or a bunch of your friends?"

"No, I came here instead of going to my prom. With a couple of girlfriends. I'd had a bad breakup with my boyfriend, so I didn't want to go to prom. We came here instead."

Michael frowned. "So you never went to your prom?"

Natalie shook her head. "Naw."

"But you ought to be a pro at skating." Michael flawlessly skated around the rink backward and stopped when he reached her again.

Natalie started to skate and now tried to pick up her own speed, feeling the need to put forth a better effort. Within a minute, she was finding an easy groove. And before long, she was moving her feet with a flair that she had when she used to roller-skate years ago.

And then she stumbled, and fell on her butt.

Michael immediately skated over to her. "I guess that's what I get for acting like I'm still eighteen."

Michael extended his hand. "Falling's part of the fun. As long as you're okay. Are you okay?"

"I'm fine." Natalie took his hand, allowed her to pull him up. As she got to her feet, she stumbled slightly. He pulled her more forcefully, and she landed against his chest. The momentum caused both of them to lose their footing, but Michael steeled his strong arms and kept them both on their feet.

The feel of his chest against her breasts, as well as his muscular arms wrapped around her, caused Natalie's stomach to flutter. Being in this man's arms felt so good....

"I told you I'd catch you," Michael said, and before Natalie knew what was happening, he planted his mouth on hers.

Heat exploded within her body, and Natalie purred. Then she slid her hands up that magnificent chest and looped her arms around his neck.

She surrendered to the kiss in the truest sense of the word. Opening her mouth wide, she allowed him better access. His tongue swept into her mouth, touching hers in the most sensual way.

Natalie tightened her arms around his neck. Michael pressed his palms into her back and urged her closer. And as they stood there, kissing to an Eric B and Rakim song, Michael's hands went down to her bottom. As he pulled her body against his, Natalie felt the evidence of his desire for her.

He was hard.

And she, too, was flushed with sexual desire. She wanted him, no doubt about it.

Michael was the one to break the kiss. He looked down at her, his heavy breaths mingling with hers.

"Would it bother you if I said that I wanted to…"

A zap of heat struck Natalie's private region. "Wanted to what?"

Michael framed her face gently, then kissed her forehead. "Don't worry. No matter how much I want to, I'm going to refrain. I want you to know that this is about getting to know you, not getting in your pants."

Strangely, Natalie felt a sense of disappointment.

Michael pressed his fingers into her waist, and another sexual charge swept through her. Then he asked, "Want to get something to eat?"

"Hmm?" It seemed like such an odd question, given that they'd just been all hot and heavy.

"If I'm going to stop touching you, I need to do something else with my hands. They've got hot dogs and pizza and popcorn here. Not the healthiest of food, but hey, it goes with the whole roller-skating experience."

"Right," Natalie said softly. "Sure."

Michael gave her a questioning look. "Disappointed?" he asked.

"No. Of course not." But her words were hardly convincing.

Michael placed his finger beneath her chin and tilted her face upward. Then he kissed her again, slow and sweet.

"If you're free tomorrow evening, I'd love to give you a night you'll never forget. Are you game?"

"Yes," Natalie responded immediately.

She had no clue what Michael had in mind. But she knew that she wanted to find out....

Chapter 14

Natalie could hardly sleep that evening, as she was still on a high from her date with Michael. He certainly was a gentleman. Spending time with him, nothing about him said "player" to her. He'd been considerate, sweet, funny and thoughtful.

And romantic.

They'd enjoyed hot dogs, popcorn and soda, and then had proceeded to hold hands as they skated to some slow jams. She and Michael had shared more kisses, and when they'd finally left Roller Palace, Natalie was sorry that she hadn't been leaving in Michael's car.

She had wanted to be close to him for a little longer. Maybe even share some more kisses.

But there was always today. Another date that Michael told her would be a surprise. But this time, instead of meeting him at his restaurant, she was allowing him to pick her up at her uncle's place.

"Another date," Deanna said, grinning from ear to ear as she sat on the sofa in the living room, looking out the window for Michael's car.

"I don't know why you're so happy about it," Natalie said wryly.

"Because *you're* happy. It's like you've all but forgotten about Vance. And that's a good thing."

Natalie couldn't argue with that. "That's true." And then she shrugged. "I don't know what's going to happen, but I know that with him, I feel alive and happy. I never thought I'd feel this way so soon after my divorce."

"It's a little early for a dinner date," Deanna commented, glancing at the clock. "I wonder what he's got planned for four in the afternoon."

"I don't know." Natalie fastened the last strap of her two shoes. "It's a surprise."

"It's exciting. Make sure you text me when you get to wherever you're going."

"Okay," Natalie said. Then, "I can't believe we haven't heard from Nigel yet. I thought he would have had something to report back from Rodney Cook."

"Don't even worry about any of that right now," Deanna told her. "Just worry about your—" She stopped abruptly. "Ooh, there he is!" Deanna exclaimed, getting onto her knees on the sofa as she pulled one shade to the side to get a better look.

Natalie couldn't help reflecting on how she and Deanna were getting along so well now. Ten years apart, and now they were being the sisters to each other in the true sense of the word. If only it hadn't taken the death of their aunt to get them to this point.

"I'll see you later," Natalie told her.

"Should I wait up?" Deanna asked with a playful glint in her eye.

"Sis, you are too much!" Natalie said with a giggle. Then she opened the door.

"Have fun!" Deanna called out to her.

Natalie didn't respond. Instead, she headed out the door and down the front steps.

Michael exited the car, and the sight of him took Natalie's breath away. Dressed in black slacks and a white dress shirt, he looked as if he had stepped off of the pages of *GQ* magazine.

But it was his smile that hit her the most. That beautiful smile that gave her butterflies.

Michael's eyes widened with pleasure as they swept over her. "Wow. You look…wow."

Natalie was wearing a little black dress, the kind that hugged her curves. It had a low V-neck which exposed her cleavage. That combined with her black stiletto heels, she knew she looked good.

Michael looped his arms around her waist and gave her a little kiss. When he was done, Natalie glanced over her shoulder at the house. Deanna, not trying to hide that she'd been spying, gave a little wave. It was a good thing Uncle Dave was out with one of his nephews, or he'd probably be out here making wedding plans.

"I'm ready if you are," Natalie said.

Michael opened the passenger car door for her, made sure she was safely inside, then closed it. Moments later, he was getting in behind the driver's wheel.

"Now, as lovely as you look—and you definitely look lovely—I took the liberty of arranging a few outfits for you to wear, since we're going somewhere real special tonight."

Natalie glanced over her shoulder to the backseat. "I don't understand."

"You'll see." Michael smiled at her as he continued to drive.

A short while later, Michael parked at a small boutique shop in downtown Cleveland, not too far from his restaurant. Cora's House of Fashion was a store Natalie had never heard of nor seen before.

"We're going in here?" Natalie asked as Michael headed toward the front door. Beautiful gowns were displayed in the window, including a stunning strapless wedding dress.

"Yep."

As Natalie followed him, she noticed something else in the window. A sign that said Closed.

"Michael, it's closed," Natalie said.

He reached for the door nonetheless, saying, "Don't worry."

She let Michael take the lead, and sure enough, the front door was unlocked. Once inside, she saw a woman, standing in the middle of the shop facing the door that appeared to be waiting for them.

"Hello, Mike." The attractive, robust woman greeted him with a warm smile. She was five foot nothing, with a caramel complexion and a set of the biggest dimples Natalie had ever seen.

"Hey, Cora." Moving toward her, Michael gave her a hug. When he eased back, he said, "Cora, this is Natalie. Natalie, this is my friend, Cora. She's a fashion designer."

"Oh, wow," Natalie said. Then she stepped toward Cora and offered the woman her hand. "It's nice to meet you."

"Are you excited?" Cora asked.

"I don't know," Natalie answered honestly. "I have no clue what's going on."

Cora glanced at Michael, giving him a questioning look. Then her eyes registered understanding. "Ahh, this evening is a surprise. Wonderful." She strolled toward a rack of gowns. In an array of colors, some were glittery, some shimmery, but they all looked gorgeous.

"Well," Cora said, delicately touching a shimmery blue

dress, "you can have your pick of any of these dresses. For your special evening."

Natalie wasn't sure she had heard correctly. Her face must have shown her confusion, because Cora nodded. Then Natalie looked at Michael, and he said, "Whichever one you like, it's yours."

"You—you're serious?"

"Very," Michael said.

Natalie whirled around and looked at him. His smile was bashful and charming.

"Michael wanted you to feel like a princess," Cora explained.

Natalie was touched. No one had ever done this for her before. Stepping closer to the rack of dresses, she saw that they ranged in color and style. From a scoop-neck black gown to a vibrant red cocktail dress, anything she could have wanted for the evening was here.

She faced Michael again. "But I don't know where we're going. So how can I know which dress to choose?"

"Choose what you like," he told her. "Because it's not about the dress. It's about the person in it."

Natalie couldn't help blushing. And she remembered their hot kisses at Roller Palace, and how Michael had made it clear he wanted her but also wanted her to know that it was about more than a sexual attraction.

Michael was doing a fantastic job of making her remember, even if only for a short time, just how special it was to feel appreciated.

And as she surveyed the various dresses once more, she did feel appreciated. And very much like a woman.

Natalie selected a floor-length black dress with the scoop-neck and low back, a red dress that had caught her eye initially and an ivory one to start with. The ivory dress hung just

elow the knee, while the red one looked a bit shorter. The
ed one was also the more formfitting of the two.

Natalie tried on the black dress first, which though absolutely lovely, she decided to rule out. It was hard to dress when you didn't know exactly where you were going, but this ne seemed perhaps a little too formal. It would be lovely for he charitable event, but perhaps not for this evening. Next, he tried on the ivory dress, which flared out at the hem and vas quite darling. But it didn't make her come alive. It was nice dress, but she just felt ordinary in it.

She had saved the red dress for last and when she put it n, she grinned. Yes, this was the dress. It was formfitting nough to show off her shape, but not too tight. The low V-neck was accented by jewels encrusted around the bosom rea. The back scooped low, adding a more feminine touch o a dress that undoubtedly made her feel like a sex kitten.

This was the kind of dress that you could wear at a cocktail party, or even a gala event, because it made a statement.

As she surveyed herself in the mirror, she drew in a deep breath. It was clear that she was going to be making a statement with this dress.

One she never thought she would want to make, certainly not until she'd been divorced for a long, long time.

And yet, she was ready to flaunt her sex appeal. Because here was something special about Michael. She didn't want o question what she was feeling; she was just going to go with it and enjoy what was certain to be a wonderful evening.

"This is it," Natalie said as she exited the dressing room. She looked around for Michael, but saw only Cora.

"Mike is getting dressed in another room," Cora explained. "He'll meet up with you when you're both dressed."

"Oh." Natalie had been looking forward to seeing his reaction.

"And I agree," Cora said, "this dress is stunning on you."

Natalie did a little twirl, checking herself out in the three paneled mirror. "It certainly is."

"And no dress would be complete without shoes. Not that there's anything wrong with the ones you wore here, but why not choose a pair that will go perfectly with your dress?"

"You don't have to twist my arm," Natalie said. "I *love* shoes."

Cora led her to another room, where an array of sexy shoes was displayed. Sparkly silver shoes. Black stilettos encrusted with jewels. Leopard print pumps. More classic pump designs. They all took her breath away.

But to go with the beautiful red dress she had chosen, Natalie knew she had to go all out to complete the outfit. So this time, instead of trying on a number of shoes, she went with the first pair that had caught her eye. A leopard print open slingback pump with red accents. The base area of the shoe was red, as was the four-inch heel.

"That one." She pointed to the delectable looking shoe. "Definitely that one."

Natalie tried on her size. And she felt the way Cinderella must have felt when the glass slipper was put on her foot with ease. This shoe was made for her.

"Oh, my goodness," she said when she saw her reflection. She looked hot. Not sophisticated and sexy, but hot. She was already trying to imagine Michael's reaction to her.

"So, do you know Michael well?" Natalie asked Cora.

"He's friends with my brother," Cora explained. "And thanks to his generosity, I was able to open this store. I don't make the shoes or purses, but all of the dresses are my original designs."

"Your work is incredible."

Cora beamed. "Thanks. Michael thought so, too, which is why he agreed to invest in my business. This is a dream come true for me. He's really a sweetheart."

"Sounds like it," Natalie said. Even what he had done for her today showed that he put thought into his actions. He had planned a Cinderella-type experience for her and so far she was loving every moment of it.

"Oh. My. Goodness."

At the sound of Michael's voice, Natalie turned. Her breath left her lungs in a rush when she saw him in a tailored navy suit, and a white dress shirt that was open at the collar.

That body, that smile… He was absolutely scrumptious.

"You're looking quite lovely yourself," she said, her voice raspy.

He walked toward her. "I'm the luckiest guy in the world, that's for sure."

"I can't believe you did all this for me," Natalie said.

Michael stroked her cheek. "If you're impressed with this, wait till you see what's next."

Natalie left the boutique feeling the way Cinderella must have felt. She looked beautiful. And she had a Prince Charming who was taking her out for a wonderful evening.

No one had splurged on her like this before. Yes, Vance had spent a lot of money on her, buying her gowns and shoes and jewelry, but those grand gestures had never seemed to come from the heart the way Michael's actions did.

"Where's the car—" The words died on Natalie's lips when she realized that the stretch Hummer limo was where Michael's car had been. "No…that's not for us, is it?"

Michael took her hand and walked with her to the black limousine. "Yesterday, you told me that you never went to your prom because you'd broken up with your boyfriend."

"I told you that?" Natalie wondered when she'd blabbed, then it came to her. And she was even more touched that Michael had not only paid attention to her comment, but had planned this because of it.

She hated to keep drawing comparisons to Vance, but maybe they were necessary. Because she had all but written Michael off simply because he was a professional athlete. But Vance would have paid no attention to a comment like that, much less planned something special for her because of it. In fact, he had shown no interest in her family. When she told him they were estranged and why, he hadn't expressed any remorse on her behalf. Instead, he'd said, "People need to get over this kind of nonsense. It shows you who your real friends are, even when it comes to family. Better to not stay in touch with them, anyway, because now they might want to make amends only because you're married to someone with loads of cash."

Surprised at his words, Natalie had said nothing, but her heart had hurt at his comment. First, it hadn't escaped her that he saw his money as his money alone, even though they were married. It was the kind of attitude that could cause problems in a marriage. But mostly, she'd been disappointed in his reaction to her estrangement from her family. He had encouraged her to keep her distance, when maybe what she'd needed was somebody to help persuade her after all these years to do the right thing—which was to make amends with her sister and her family. Because now that she was here in Cleveland, doing just that, she felt one hundred percent better.

"You told me yesterday," Michael said.

"Yes, that's right. I appreciate you even caring."

"Of course I care."

She believed him. "Seriously," Natalie said, "today has been…extraordinary."

Michael opened the door to the limo for her. "And it's not finished yet."

Natalie had no clue where they were going, but she was enjoying holding Michael's hand in the backseat of the limo.

Soon she saw that they were heading toward Lake Erie. And as the limo drove past the pier, heading away from the popular waterfront restaurants, Natalie became curious.

"Michael? Where are we going?"

"You'll see."

The suspense was nearly killing her. The driver kept going, entering a marina. And when he came to a stop, saying, "This is as far as I can take you," Natalie figured they must be going out on a boat.

"Are we going on a boat ride?" Natalie asked. "Some sort of dinner cruise?"

"Probably a little nicer than a *boat ride*."

They exited the limo, and Michael took her hand. Natalie's eyes scanned the marina with excitement.

"Which one?" Natalie asked. "Which boat is it?"

"You'll see."

Natalie tried not to act overly excited, tried to maintain her cool composure. But given the fact that she and Michael were both dressed to the nines, she couldn't help staring at the large yachts. It stood to reason that Michael was probably going to take her out on one of the nicer vessels.

Her eyes locked on the largest yacht, which was all white, its body gleaming as though it was brand-new. And as they got closer and she heard the sounds of music and saw that indeed they were coming from the largest yacht in the form of a live band, she let out a little squeal.

"Excited, are you?" Michael asked.

"Michael, you don't know how much I've always wanted to go on the water. But with Vance…" Her voice trailed off. She didn't want to mention Vance, nor even think of him. He deserved none of her thoughts.

"Forget Vance," she went on. "All I can say is that I've always wanted to go boating, and if we are about to get onto that fabulous-looking yacht…" She squeezed Michael's hand tighter.

"Indeed, we are."

Natalie squealed again, this time adding a little giddy jump. And she couldn't help wondering how she had so quickly gone from not wanting a relationship with Michael to being more than ready to explore every possibility with him.

She didn't have the answer for that, but she knew that tonight she was not going to question what she was feeling. She was simply going to go with it. Because she was feeling incredible and alive—and loving it.

After all, even while married, she had not been able to say that she truly felt happy and alive most of the time.

And it wasn't that she was naïve enough to expect to be happy *all* of the time, but she had felt Vance slipping away. She had sensed that he wasn't totally committed to their marriage. She knew that he was into the flash and pomp of being a professional athlete—and that included the adoration of all those female fans. The truth was, she wasn't surprised to learn that he had cheated on her. The only surprise had been learning that it had been with her supposed best friend.

"Michael Jones!"

At the sound of his name, Michael turned. So did Natalie. And there stood a woman, grinning widely. She had dark brown skin and long, thin braids. Her shapely figure was highlighted with tight jeans and a cotton top that looked a size or two too small.

The woman took a step forward. "That is you, isn't it?" the woman said. "Oh, my God." She jutted out her hand to shake his. "I'm such a huge fan. I've watched you since you started playing for Cleveland, and I think you're amazing."

The woman was standing with another female, one who seemed a little bashful. She was saying nothing, while her friend looked so excited she might die.

"Thank you," Michael said, his tone curt.

The woman extended a notepad. "Would you mind signing this for me?"

"Actually," Michael began, "this isn't the time. I'm trying to enjoy a private moment."

"It's okay," Natalie said. "Go ahead and sign it for the lady."

Michael took the pad and the pen that the woman extended, and Natalie noticed an almost sense of irritation on his part as he signed his name for her. He wasn't the cordial man she had seen with other fans at his restaurant. She figured it was because this woman's attention was taking away from their romantic evening together, but that was part of being a public person. You had to expect that people would approach you in public when they saw you.

"Now if you'll excuse me," Michael said tersely, and took Natalie by the elbow. He led her toward the yacht, which had the name *My Dream* painted on the side in a cursive font. He continued holding her, helping her up the plank.

When she got onto the boat, she turned. And that's when she noticed that the fan was still standing there. In fact, she waved.

Michael saw Leanne wave, and silently cursed. She was standing there, staring at him and Natalie.

Stalking him.

How had she even known he would be going out on his yacht? Had she been following him, or simply waiting here, knowing he would at one point show up?

Knowing Leanne, she had been frequenting the marina often, and when she saw the activity on Michael's boat, had known he would be showing up today. Between the caterers and the musicians, it would have been obvious.

At least Michael was safely on the boat with Natalie, but

he would make sure to have the captain raise the plank just in case. He didn't want any surprises from the woman he had once been fool enough to date.

After all, it was becoming clear that the woman's obsession with him would never end. Here she was, accosting him under the guise of being a fan. She knew full well that he would have to play along with her act—or else confess to Natalie how he really knew her.

And he wasn't about to identify Leanne as someone else he'd been involved with, at least not at that moment. Not when Natalie had been so wary about trusting him.

Like so many others, Leanne had had delusions of "the good life" with Michael. That had become obvious shortly after he'd met her at his restaurant, and gone out with her a few times. She was interested in his car, where he lived and the dollar figure of his latest contract. She had dressed in provocative outfits when they'd gone out, and had quickly tried to offer herself up for his pleasure in the front seat of his car.

Michael didn't want to explain his relationship with Leanne to Natalie, not at anytime. It might lead Natalie to feel more insecure, given what her husband had done.

And thus far, Leanne had been harmless, more a nuisance than anything else.

Michael could only hope that now that she had seen him with someone else, she would have the good sense to leave him alone.

Chapter 15

"This is absolutely stunning," Natalie said as she gazed around the midlevel deck of the yacht where they had stepped off of the plank. She saw sleek mahogany paneling and floors. The seating area, which resembled a living room, had cream-colored leather sofas. From the furniture to the decor, everything about this room was exquisite, and looked as if it could be featured in a magazine.

But it was the other decor touches that got to Natalie: the vases of fresh red roses in almost every corner, the glowing candles. Clearly, Michael had taken the time and effort to make the boat just right for their evening.

"Something about being on a yacht makes me want to be barefoot," Michael said. He sat on one of the sofas and began to unlace his Italian designer shoes. "You?"

"Sure." Natalie sat across from him. His eyes were fixed to her hands and feet as she undid the buckles and slipped out of the shoes. "Actually, that feels really good. As much as I love shoes, wearing a new pair can be painful."

Michael got to his feet, and so did she. She looked out at the marina. It was a warm summer evening, with just the hint of a breeze. She imagined that setting sail on a day like this would be ideal.

Michael snaked his arms around her waist from behind. "Want to see the downstairs?"

Natalie's heart fluttered. She knew what was downstairs. The sleeping quarters.

She nodded, knowing that Michael simply wanted to give her the grand tour. Michael continued to hold her from behind as he led her downstairs. There, she saw a decent-size kitchen, where a man dressed in a black suit and white gloves was opening the fridge. Seeing Natalie and Michael, he nodded in greeting.

Michael didn't take his hands off of her, and the intimacy of how he was touching her made her heart beat faster. He guided her through another living area, bigger than the one above. This one was complete with a large-screen television, and plush cream-colored carpeting that felt wonderful beneath her feet. There was also a dining room, with a table set for two. Again, candles were glowing around a red rose centerpiece.

Michael led her toward a cluster of doors, all of them closed. With one hand pressed against her stomach, he opened the first door with his other hand. "This is one bedroom," he explained, his lips close to her ear. "Small, but nice."

A tingling sensation spread down the length of Natalie's arms. "Yes, very nice. And a good use of space with the bunk bed."

"Uh-huh." Michael's deep voice caused a shiver of pleasure to wash over her. Then, continuing to walk with her body in front of his, he went to the next door, which was to the left.

Opening it, he said, "This is the bathroom. Glass shower, marble countertops, enough space to move around."

"It's gorgeous." It was the kind of bathroom she would expect to find in a high-end hotel.

He showed her the next bedroom, which was large enough to hold a queen bed. And then he opened the last door.

"And this is the master suite."

As Natalie's eyes took in the room, she could see why this was the master suite. While the previous bedroom had been beautiful, this one was spectacular. It also had a queen-size bed, one that had rose petals scattered over the bronze-colored bedding. One entire wall had a window, which let in a lot of light. On that same wall, beneath the window, was a desk. This room had another flat-screen television. It didn't look at all like a room that was on a boat.

Michael took a step forward, the pressure of his large thigh forcing her to advance into the room. "Walk-in closet," he said, gesturing to the open door on the left. "And take a look at this bathroom."

The bathroom was large. It had his and hers sinks, sophisticated faucets and marble countertops. There was a Jacuzzi tub beneath the window, and also a glass shower easily big enough to hold two people.

"This is even more beautiful than I imagined a yacht could be," Natalie said.

"I liked this one because it isn't enormously big, but it's still a great size. We could be comfortable sailing to the Caribbean…or anywhere else."

Now Natalie turned in his arms. "We?"

"I would take you anywhere you wanted to go."

I want to be right here. Exhaling a shuddery breath, Natalie stepped away from Michael's arms and took a closer look at the painting on the wall. It was a tasteful nude of a black couple in an embrace.

It made her think about her and Michael getting naked....

Suddenly, Michael was directly behind her again, his hand slipping around her waist. She loved how his flat palm felt on her belly.

"I bought that at a gallery in Atlanta. Beautiful, isn't it?"

"Yes." Natalie's voice was faint.

"I don't want you to think I'm being presumptuous," Michael began, lowering his lips to her ear, "but in case you wanted to stay out on the lake tonight, we can sleep here."

"We can?" Again, she sounded breathless.

"Yeah." Now Michael's own voice was barely above a whisper. "I'm not gonna lie—I would love nothing more than for us to share the night."

His words sent a thrill of desire tingling down her spine.

"But there are other bedrooms here, as you've seen, and I'm more than happy to sleep in one of them—if that's what you'd—"

Natalie spun around so fast that Michael's words died in his throat. She slipped her arms around his shoulders, rose up onto her toes and planted her mouth on his. It was unexpected, and it was amazing.

The feel of his full lips brought dizzying sensations. The man was gorgeous. His wide shoulders and muscled chest, his thick, strong arms... She explored it all with her fingers as her mouth worked over his.

The kissing was slow, mostly their mouths moving over each other's, with the occasional flick of the tongue and a suckle on her bottom lip that drove her wild. But when Michael pulled back to look at her, and she saw the heat in his eyes, they came together again in a full fury of passion. Their mouths collided with an electric charge, both of their lips parting so that their tongues could play over each other's. His tongue felt warm over hers it tasted incredible.

Lowering both of her hands, Natalie pressed her fingers

into the thick wall of Michael's chest, knowing without doubt that she needed to feel this man's naked skin beneath her hands.

Beneath her body. On top of her body. Behind her body.

Every which way she could have him.

She had a raging lust for this man, and she didn't know why. It was so shocking that it startled her.

Michael's hands moved down her back, and she purred into his mouth when his hands came back up her sides, his fingers skimming the sides of her dress that led to her breasts. She wanted him to take the dress off, rip this expensive garment from her body and take her right here on this bed.

But instead, he tore his lips from hers and looked down at her with a dazed expression.

"Upstairs. On the top deck. I told Pierre that once we got on board, he should get the dinner ready for us."

Pierre… Natalie was almost stunned to realize that she and Michael were not the only two people in the universe, that's how wrapped up in him she had been.

"Of course," she said. "And whatever's cooking smells amazing."

"And the captain is waiting for word from me as to when to set sail. I was originally thinking we could eat while we were out on the water, but now…" His voice trailed off.

Natalie knew what he was thinking. And she was thinking the same thing. "You want to eat now *before* we set sail…so we can send everybody except the captain home once we're done."

"You read my mind," Michael said.

"I'm not a mind reader, but what we're both feeling… It's obvious we're on the same page. In fact, if you want to send everyone home right now…"

"Pierre is only here to ensure that the meal is warm and serve it, but I paid the musicians for the next four hours."

"And if you send them home early, they'll be really happy." She paused. "And so will we." Natalie ran her fingertips along Michael's chest, making it clear what she was getting at.

Michael's eyes twinkled as he looked at her. "When did you turn into this person?"

"You don't like it?"

"Oh, I love it." Michael gave her a kiss on the cheek. "You'll get no complaints from me."

Natalie giggled.

"I'll tell the captain to set sail for about an hour, then we'll take it from there. That way, we can enjoy eating while cruising, then decide what to do next."

"Okay." Natalie smiled bashfully. "Sounds like a plan."

They went upstairs, to the upper deck, where Michael sat her on one of the four white leather sofas. Then he went to speak the captain. A couple of minutes later, the boat started to move.

Natalie enjoyed the string quartet and the feel of the wind against her skin. The floor's surface here was gritty, like stucco, which she figured made it easier to stand on when the yacht was on the move. It was an area she could easily imagine filled with people laughing and having a good time.

As the yacht moved farther from the marina, Natalie marveled at the view. It was quite a different vantage point to look at the land from the water, to see the various establishments on the pier while she was in a completely different place. It was like looking at the world through a glass. She was on an island of serenity, while the world went on around her.

Just like in the lower cabin, there was a table on this deck. But it was a more casual table. Lower, with leather sofa-style seating.

While the table could easily seat eight people, there were two place settings, side by side, complete with champagne flutes. In front of the place settings was an arrangement of red roses and two candles. This time, the candles were encased with glass so that the breeze wouldn't extinguish their flames.

Michael appeared, his face lighting up in a smile as he did. Natalie could easily get used to this. Get used to that smile warming her up every day.

"It's warm and not too breezy, so I figured we could eat out here," Michael said. "But if you'd prefer to eat down below, the table is set there, as well."

"Here's fine. Down below is beautiful, but it's more of your typical dining room. This—" She gestured to the vast lake. "This is extraordinary."

"You're extraordinary."

Pierre came up the stairs carrying a silver carafe with what looked to be a bottle of champagne. Immaculately dressed in a black suit and bow tie and white gloves, Natalie wouldn't be surprised to learn that he was fresh off of a flight from Paris.

Michael took Natalie's hand and led her to the table. As they both sat, Pierre placed the carafe on the table. Then he lifted the champagne bottle, opened it with a pop, to which Natalie clapped, and then proceeded to pour some for both Michael and Natalie.

"Good evening, sir and madame. I want to give you your dinner choices for the evening. There are two. The first is a grilled lobster tail, with rice pilaf, and the second choice is a chicken marsala made with a wine sauce and topped with Portobello mushrooms. To start, there's tomato soup and Caesar salad."

Natalie looked at Michael in surprise. He had certainly gone all out. Because right now, she didn't feel as though she was on a yacht. She felt as though she were in a fine dining establishment. With the array of choices available to eat, she felt as though she was lacking nothing.

"I'll have the lobster," Michael announced. "With the soup to start."

"I'll go for the chicken," Natalie said. "With the salad."

"Of course," Michael commented.

"*And* the soup," Natalie went on. She shrugged. "I'm famished."

The quartet began to play a peppier classical tune. The ambience was beyond lovely. As far as Natalie was concerned, this was romance at its finest. Natalie wholeheartedly believed that Michael genuinely liked her.

The quartet played all through dinner, and after a dessert of crème brûlée, Michael stood from the table and took Natalie's hand in his. "May I have this dance?"

Natalie stood. She looked toward the shoreline, which was so far off it seemed like it was another world. But she could see the twinkling lights of the boardwalk and its various restaurants, which was a beautiful sight to behold.

Natalie savored the feeling of Michael's arms around her waist, and she leaned close as they danced, resting her head against his shoulder. When she tipped her head back to look up at him, he smiled down at her.

"You're incredibly beautiful." His voice was low, barely a whisper. "You're like no one I've ever known before."

Natalie couldn't help thinking that just weeks ago, she would have dismissed the comment as the kind of easy line that men like Michael—players—threw around with ease. But now, in his arms like this, she totally believed him.

"You're something pretty special yourself," she told him.

And then he moved his hands from her waist to her face, where he gently stroked her skin with his fingers. The light feelings brought out the most blissful sensations. And when he put his mouth on hers, it felt like heaven.

He held her, swayed his body with hers to the music as their lips mated. And then, his hands ventured from her face and down her arms to capture both of her hands. He held

hem at the sides of their bodies as they continued to move
n a seductive rhythm.

Finally, Michael tore his lips from Natalie's, and she pro-
ested with a little gasp. "We're getting closer to shore."

Natalie snaked her arms around his waist as she turned to
look at the marina. "Mmm-hmm."

"Hey," Michael said softly. She looked up at him, which
was what he wanted. He could never get enough of looking at
her face. She was so incredibly beautiful. Her lips were moist
from their kiss, and her bright eyes were alive with sensuality.

He needed to make her his.

But not yet. Not until they were back at the shore. He was
glad he'd told the captain to start heading back before they'd
started their desserts. Because Michael couldn't wait until
they could send Pierre and the musicians home.

So he danced with Natalie. Enjoyed smoothing his hands
over the curves of her hips. Enjoyed the feel of her soft breasts
pressed against his chest. Enjoyed that radiant smile of hers
and her infectious laugh.

Finally, they arrived back at the marina, and Michael saw
the waiter and musicians off of the yacht and instructed the
captain to set sail again. When he returned to Natalie, she
was sitting on one of the sofas on the upper deck with her feet
tucked under her. But one foot was slightly exposed, and he
could see the vibrant red polish on her toes.

She looked so darn delectable. And he was aroused.

Making his way back over to her, he led her down from
the upper deck to the lower cabin. Pierre had opened a bottle
of champagne and left it in the master suite, as per his in-
struction, and it sat on the night table beside the bed. Beside
the carafe of champagne was a box of gourmet chocolates.
Michael's plan had been to feed them to her as a prelude to
lovemaking.

But now that he was here, crossing the threshold to the

bedroom with her, the last thing he wanted to do with Natalie was sip champagne and dine on fine chocolates.

Instead, he wanted to dine on her.

Natalie looked over her shoulder at him. "When—"

"I thought of everything," he told her, interrupting the question.

"You certainly have," Natalie said, stroking his face.

And then she took a step backward. An invitation, most definitely. He saw it in her eyes, even if he were to have somehow missed the obvious slipping of her hand beneath the shoulder of one strap of the dress.

Michael moved toward her with a growl. She was breathtaking. Beautiful both inside and out. Any man who could dump her certainly needed a lobotomy.

He walked toward her, placed his hand on hers, feeling the delicate silky material of her dress and wanting nothing more than to rip it off.

"I hope I met your requirements," Michael said. Natalie looked up at him with a question in her eyes. "You said you wanted me to give you a different kind of a date, not the typical expensive dinner that didn't require much thought," he explained. "So I hope—"

Michael stopped talking when Natalie suddenly eased up and placed her lips on the side of his jaw. She suckled his flesh softly, and damn, his entire body felt a rush of heat. He couldn't remember ever having been so attracted to anyone, so fiercely needing someone in his bed.

"This was more than I could have ever dreamed of," Natalie told him. "You've surprised me in the best possible way."

She brought her lips to his opposite jaw, and this time he groaned as her tongue flicked over his skin. "Natalie…"

"Now, I hope you don't mind if we skip the champagne and chocolate for now. Not that I'm not impressed. But I was kind of thinking that we've been waiting a long time for this moment. All that time on the lake, enjoying a wonderful dinner. The entire time, I couldn't stop thinking about…" Her words ended on a shrug, but he knew exactly what she had been thinking.

Because he had been thinking the exact same thing.

He swept his hand into her hair, tugging on it gently to tip her head back as his mouth claimed hers. The sensations flowing through him made his head swim. He wanted nothing more than to feel her legs wrapped around his waist, but first, he wanted to please her. Tease her so exquisitely that she would forget having been with any other man.

As he reached for the zipper under the arm of her dress, he knew that pleasing her would be paramount to even pleasing himself. Knowing that he made her sigh with pleasure and moan his name over and over again would be his greatest reward.

She wasn't shy as he let the dress fall from her body to the floor. She had on a strapless black bra embroidered with lace, and delicate lace panties that matched.

Michael's eyes swept over her, slowly, taking in the sight of an exquisite beauty he knew he would always appreciate. Natalie was like a fine piece of art. How was he so lucky to have her with him right now?

He brought his mouth to hers again, his tongue flicking over hers as he reached for the clasp on the strapless bra and loosened it. Not pulling his mouth from hers, he continued to kiss her, enjoying swallowing her sighs of pleasure as his hands moved from her back to her breasts. He covered the full mounds with his palms, savoring the feel of the erect tips pressing against the palms of his hands.

But it was when she slipped her arms around his neck and whispered, "Make love to me, Michael," that he kissed her so ferociously as if to permanently meld her lips to his. Nothing had tasted as good as the taste of her tongue in his mouth.

Nothing had felt as good as her body in his arms. He tweaked her nipples, suckled on her tongue as her mouth opened with rapture and all she could do was pant in delight.

Kissing her wasn't enough. So he lowered his head to one breast, where he circled the tip of his tongue around her nipple, and was rewarded when she gripped his shoulder blades almost violently.

"Oh, baby…"

He teased her like that, pressing the tip of his tongue back and forth over her swollen peak, driving her crazy. He loved how she responded to him, loved knowing that he was bringing her pleasure. He brought his mouth to her other nipple and continued his loving assault. When her knees buckled, he scooped his arms around her waist and held her up. And then he carried her to the bed where he laid her down carefully. She looked up at him with heavy-lidded eyes.

"My God," he said, his throat thick with emotion. "You are such a vision."

She reached for his hand, and he took it in his and kissed the inside of her wrist. Then he released her hand so that he could begin to shed his own clothes. Off with his jacket blazer, and then off with his dress shirt. He loosened his pants, letting them fall to the floor.

His erection was straining against his boxers, and he saw Natalie's eyes move over him from head to toe. Her eyes widened with excitement, which pleased him.

She stretched out so that she could extend her hand and stroke his inner thigh. The feathery light touch drove him wild. "Come here."

Michael needed no further encouragement. He lay on the bed beside Natalie, his hand cradling her face as he kissed her again. It was a slow kiss filled with meaning. It was something Michael wasn't used to, and in many ways it caught him off guard. Because what he was about to experience with

Natalie right now was far more significant than any other activity he had experienced with other women.

Somehow, it was different.

He stroked her breasts again, feeling more carnal heat when she moaned long and hard. His hands moved down her flat stomach to the edge of her panties. He paused there, as if seeking permission. He wanted everything to be right.

"Please," Natalie rasped.

Michael positioned himself on his knees so that he was able to take her panties off her body. He shimmied them down her shapely thighs and down her strong calves. Her beautiful legs. My God. Those delicate feet with those red-painted toenails.

He thought again just how lucky he was. And as he tossed the delicate garment onto the floor, then his eyes ventured to the center of her womanhood. Everything about her was gorgeous. He kissed her calves and then continued kissing the inner portion of her legs until he reached her thighs. Then, taking one of her hands in his, he met her eyes again, saw her parted lips and the look of raw desire on her face. And then he delicately touched her center with his other hand, feeling a rush when she moaned in response. He put his mouth where his fingers had been, and her moans grew even greater.

Delicately, exquisitely, he pleasured her until she was crying out his name. Only then did he kiss a path to her torso, suckle each breast, then continue to her mouth. She was panting, begging him to take her.

He kissed her, kissed her until he felt her shudder beneath him. And only then did he reach for the night table drawer and open it. It was where he had put the condoms earlier. He got up from the bed and hastily stripped out of his boxers and rolled the condom over his shaft. And when he looked at Natalie, her lips still parted, her breathing still ragged, but a smile lighting up that beautiful face, he joined her on the bed again, settled between her thighs and entered her.

"Oh!" she cried, gripping his back.

He moved slowly, withdrawing and then filling her, causing her to gasp.

"Oh, baby," she purred.

Michael fondled her breast. "Baby...I love how that sounds."

"I love how you're making me feel."

He kissed her, devouring her mouth as he thrust into her. Natalie moaned, wrapped her legs tightly around him. Michael picked up speed, encouraged by every one of her sighs. He made love to her with a maddening rhythm, claiming her in the most primal of ways.

Soon, he felt her tense beneath him. He continued his pleasurable assault. Then Natalie's fingers were pressing even harder into his back, and she was arching her body, and crying out his name.

He kissed her as she climaxed, this time slowly and sweetly. "Yes, baby," he said. "That's it."

And as she quivered in his arms, he continued to love her until his own orgasm claimed him.

When their heavy breathing began to subside, Michael eased up so that he could look at her. Meeting his eyes, she gently placed her hand on his face.

"A pretty good start," he said.

Natalie raised an eyebrow. "Good start?"

"Uh-huh. Because I'm not even close to being done with you yet." Michael paused. "Got a problem with that?"

Natalie grinned. "Not at all."

Chapter 16

Natalie's eyes fluttered open. She had a sense of disorientation, immediately knowing she wasn't in her own bed, but not knowing where she was.

And then she remembered. She was on the boat. With Michael.

Her eyes opened fully, and there was his smiling face. Her eyes went from his face and that killer smile to his naked torso. Almost instantly she felt a flush of heat, remembering what they'd done in his bedroom out on the open water.

"Good morning," she said.

"I made breakfast."

Natalie sat up, and the blanket that had been pulled up over her chest slipped down. She, like Michael, was topless.

She saw his eyes wander from her face to her breasts, and she felt another flush of heat. No need to be bashful. The man had tantalized every part of her body the night before.

"Are we still out on the lake?"

"No, we're back at the shore. The captain has left, and it's just me and you. I went out and picked up a few things while you were sleeping."

"You did?"

"Just eggs and some fresh fruit. I already had coffee on the boat." He leaned close, kissed her cheek. "But during breaks between lovemaking last night, you said something about really liking omelets."

"I did?"

Michael flicked his tongue over her earlobe, and although they'd spent much of the night naked and wrapped around each other, Natalie was ready to make love to him again.

"Yep. I asked you what you liked for breakfast, and you said an omelet with ham, onions, red peppers and cheese."

"And you remembered?" She barely remembered her own name, not after the amazing sensual experience she had shared with Michael.

"I remember everything."

The deep timbre of his voice made it clear he wasn't just talking about their conversations, but about everything she had enjoyed while in his arms.

She placed her hand on his thigh, close to his shaft. "You keep that up, and we're not going to get to eat breakfast for a while. And I think it might be a good idea for us to have some sustenance. For energy…"

Grinning, Michael eased back. "True enough."

Natalie could easily imagine being on this boat with Michael for days and days as they traveled to the Caribbean and beyond. Being here with him was like being in a different world. She had forgotten all about the problems in her life.

Suddenly, she leaned forward and gave him a kiss on the lips. It was a soft kiss, but it quickly deepened.

Michael pulled away from her, moaning. "We can't let the breakfast get cold.

"No. You're right. After all, we've got the rest of the day to do each other."

Michael's eyes widened. "Ooh, I love it when you talk dirty."

"Well, we don't *have* to eat right now." When had she turned into this vixen?

"Yes, we do." Michael headed for the door. "I want you to see that I'm a good cook. Then you might not want to get rid of me."

And then he was out the door, leaving Natalie pondering his comment. Right now, getting rid of him was the last thing on her mind. In fact...

In fact what? As the reality of her thought hit her, her heart began to thud. Had she so quickly developed strong feelings for him?

Before she could answer her silent question, Michael returned with a tray on which there was an omelet that looked as though it had been professionally made. Thick, filled with vegetables, pieces of ham and melted cheese. Fresh orange slices adorned the side of the plate, as well as strawberries and kiwi.

"Wow," Natalie began, her mouth watering slightly as she eyed the feast. "You've really outdone yourself."

Michael leaned forward and kissed her forehead, his thick lips sending a shiver of desire down her body. "I told you that when you're with me I'll spoil you. I'm a man of my word."

Natalie took a bite of the omelet and moaned in delight. "Mmm. This is good."

"I'm glad you like it."

Natalie heard the distinctive ring of her iPhone. Michael glanced around, in the direction of her purse. "Leave it," she said, not wanting anything to interrupt this moment with Michael. When it stopped ringing, she asked, "Where's your

breakfast? Don't tell me you made this for me and made nothing for yourself?"

"Scoot over," he told her.

Natalie scooted over with the tray on her lap, and Michael
once again exited the room. As Michael disappeared, her
phone rang again, and Natalie wondered if one of her sisters
was trying to reach her. But she made no move to get her
purse. Whatever it was could wait.

A minute later, Michael returned with his own tray, with
a similar-looking omelet, and two cups of coffee. On the side
of the tray were a sugar bowl and some creamers.

"I didn't know how you like your coffee, but here's anything you need."

Natalie smiled at him. He truly was a romantic man. So
much different than her husband had been. If Vance had ever
done anything like this for her, she would have wondered if
a Martian had invaded his body.

"I see you certainly make sure your women get the royal
treatment."

"Not wom*en*," Michael said, his expression becoming more
serious. "*You.* I hope you don't think I do this for everyone,
because I don't. And that's the truth. I'm not saying I've never
been romantic in the past, because it's my nature. But you're
different. I want to do everything to please you."

Michael's words held a double meaning, and Natalie's most
private place thrummed, remembering just how much Michael had pleased her the night before.

"How did you learn to cook like this?" That was a safe
question. She knew she was avoiding the seriousness of what
he'd said, but she wasn't yet ready to deal with what they were
truly feeling for each other. "You really have a knack for it."

"My mother," Michael explained. "She was a great cook,
and she took wonderful care of me."

Natalie stopped chewing as she met his gaze. *"Was?"*

Natalie's phone rang again, and this time she frowned. "This is the third time, isn't it?"

"Yeah," Natalie said softly. "I better see who's trying to reach me. Do you mind?"

Michael hopped off the bed, grabbed her purse and tossed it to her. Natalie retrieved her phone, and when she saw Callie's number, she quickly pressed the talk button.

"Hey, Callie," Natalie said.

"Where are you?" Callie asked.

"I'm...I'm out." She noticed Michael walk out of the room, clearly to give her privacy. "What's up?"

Callie sighed. "I wanted to give you the update. Nigel spoke with Rodney Cook."

Natalie's stomach fluttered. "And?"

"And there was some good news, but ultimately it's bad news."

Natalie frowned. "What does that mean?"

"Well, after playing games, asking for special favors before giving up any information, Rodney finally said that he knew where our mother was."

"That's excellent!" Natalie exclaimed.

"*Was* being the key word."

"If we know where she was, that can still be a clue."

"Not really," Callie said. "Let me give you the whole story. Rodney said that our mother was living in Philadelphia last he'd heard. Even though she'd tried to escape him, he knew she had friends in Philly, and it turned out that's where she went. The problem is, Nigel looked into it, and she's not there now. We're three years too late."

Natalie was silent as the words registered. "That can't be. No, there must be some sign of her. Something."

"Nigel already investigated her last address in Philadelphia, and she was there. But after moving out, it's like she disappeared into thin air."

"Obviously she didn't."

"No," Callie agreed. "She didn't. But here's the problem. Rodney was out of prison three years ago, on parole, before getting sent back. He knew where our mother was. At one point, he wanted to kill her. Nat, I think we have to consider the very real possibility that he went to Philadelphia, found her and killed her. That would explain why she seemingly vanished into thin air."

"Is that what Rodney said?" Natalie countered.

"No. But it's not exactly like he's going to admit to a murder!"

"Why agree to talk to Nigel at all?" Natalie asked. "I mean if he killed our mother?"

"Because he wanted to get perks for 'cooperating' with the police," Callie explained. "I hate to say it, but I don't think there's any reason to hope anymore. And neither does Deanna. Nat, I think our mother's dead."

Once Natalie hung up with her sister, she went into the bathroom, where she sat on the edge of the tub and had a short cry.

Then she exited the bathroom, where she saw Michael sitting on the bed. "I need to leave," she said.

Michael narrowed his eyes. "What?"

"I need to go," Natalie repeated, knowing that she sounded testy.

"I thought we were going to spend the day together."

"Yeah, well, not anymore." She searched the floor for her bra.

Michael came beside her and reached for her arm, forcing her to stop. "Why the sudden change?" Michael asked. "When I left the room, you had a smile on your face. Now you're acting like I'm the enemy."

"What's changed is that my sisters think there's no point in pursuing my mother's whereabouts anymore."

"Hold up," Michael said. "You need to give me more than that."

So Natalie did. She explained everything that had happened with her mother, the clues they'd gotten via Aunt Jean's letter, and the lead from Rodney that had gotten them nowhere. "My sisters figure there's no point in searching anymore, that all we're going to learn is bad news. They think we should quit while we're ahead. Callie said that Deanna is in agreement with her, but Callie was always the one who believed our mother was never going to return, and it's like she just wants to close the book on her now. She claims that it's better for us to have the belief that she may possibly be alive, rather than learn for sure that's she's not, but I don't buy that. I *need* to know what happened to my mother. If she's dead, so be it. But I just believe, deep in my soul, that we've gotten all these clues because we're going to find her."

Michael took her hand in his and squeezed. "Wow. I'm sorry to hear that."

Natalie pulled her hand from his. "Don't be sorry. I'm going to find my mother, even if my sisters have given up on her. I'm going to Philadelphia to look for her. And don't try to stop me."

When she turned away from him, Michael placed his hand on her shoulder, forcing her to face him. "Stop you?" he asked. "Why would *I* try to stop you?"

Natalie's lips parted, but she suddenly didn't know what to say. She finally answered, "I don't want you to tell me that I'm wasting my time."

"Why would *I* tell you that?"

Because that's exactly what Vance would say.... But telling Michael that didn't seem like the right thing to do.

After years of questioning why her mother would leave and

trying to find excuses for the abandonment, Vance had tried to bring Natalie down to earth, saying that she was foolish to think her mother had wanted her and her sisters.

A mother who wants a child doesn't leave.

For Vance, it had been black-and-white. His own father had walked out on him when he was just a child. And his mother had apparently neglected him for boyfriend after boyfriend. It was one of the things that had attracted Natalie to him, his pain. She'd had her own pain, as well, and had believed whole-heartedly that together the two of them would heal each other.

What a joke that was.

"Did you hear me?" Michael asked.

Looking up at him, she realized that she had momentarily been lost in her thoughts. "I'm sorry."

"When we were at Roller Palace, I told you I'd catch you when you fell. I meant that both literally and figuratively. And right now, it's clear to me that you need support. Why would you expect me to do anything but support you?"

"Because..." Natalie paused. And then she decided to be honest. "Because that's what Vance would have done. He would have told me that I was wasting my time with this. In fact, he told me that many times when I talked about hiring a private detective to find her. And I did once. But the detective couldn't find anything. Vance told me then that I needed to get over my mother, that she abandoned me and I should forget about her. I guess I didn't expect you to say anything different...."

Michael's jaw tightened. "So after everything, you're still comparing me to Vance?"

"I'm sorry." That was all Natalie could say.

"In fact, not only do I agree with you, I want to go to Philadelphia with you."

Michael's words stumped her. "What?"

"We'll go together," Michael said.

"You're not serious."

"Completely. So don't try to stop me. I'm not going to let you go alone."

And when Natalie saw the determination in Michael's eyes, a swell of emotion filled her chest. He was serious.

And she was grateful. Because she didn't want to do this alone.

"You'd really come along with me?" she asked.

"Try and stop me."

A tear fell from her cheek. "Michael…" Stepping toward him, she wrapped her arms around him and held him tight. He felt like an anchor, the one meant to keep her safe.

"I'm so sorry. It's just that this is so important to me."

Michael smoothed his hands over her hair. "I understand something being so important to you that you'd do anything in your power to change it."

Natalie heard something in his voice that caused her to ease back and stare up at him. And as she suspected, she saw a pained look in his eyes. "Michael?"

"My mother," he explained, and stopped.

Natalie reached for his face. "What happened?"

"There was a car crash—"

"Oh, my God." Natalie exhaled sharply. "I'm so sorry."

"My mother is still alive, thank God, but not the way she used to be." Natalie saw his Adam's apple rise and fall as he swallowed, and she continued stroking his face, giving him time to go on. "She suffered a brain injury in the crash, and even though four years have passed, she's still just a shell of her former self."

"Oh, baby." Here Natalie had immediately written him off as not being able to understand her situation, when he'd gone through something devastating, as well.

"She's in a special home, and I see her as often as I can. But it hurts, you know? I've got all this money, and I'd give every penny to see my mother well again. But no matter how much I would physically do to see her well, it's not enough."

Natalie didn't know what to say. "I'm so sorry."

She saw Michael swallow again, and knew he was trying to keep his emotions in check. "It's hard to see my mother as only a shell of the woman she used to be."

"I can't imagine how horrible that is."

"She's alive, and I'm grateful for that, but it kills me to see her go through what she's having to suffer, knowing that there is nothing I can do about it. I feel powerless." When Michael paused, Natalie stroked his face again. "I'm telling you this so you know that I understand exactly what it's like to want something so badly. Our situations are different, but if I were in your shoes, I would have to do what you're doing. I would move heaven and earth to find my mother. I want to see you find your mother as much as you do."

Natalie's heart filled with an emotion she hadn't expected to feel ever again, much less so soon after her divorce from Vance.

She was feeling love.

"I believe you," she told him. "I know you mean everything you're saying."

Michael offered her a small smile, but there was still pain in his eyes. She wished she could erase it.

"So what's your plan?" Michael asked. "We can leave here, get changed, then head to the airport. Or we can drive. I've got an Escalade at home. It's big, and comfortable."

"Depending on what we learn, we might have to drive somewhere else. Maybe even another state. So I think driving is a good idea."

"That's what I think," Michael said. "I love to drive, and Philadelphia isn't all that far. We can make it by tonight."

They could. And this way, Natalie would have someone

with her. She wouldn't even have to tell her sisters what she was doing until she got some results.

"As long as you're sure," Natalie said.

Holding her gaze, Michael said, "I'm in this with you. Whatever it takes, we'll find your mother."

And then Natalie had to swallow to keep her own emotions under control. Because a big part of her wanted to cry happy tears.

Because it truly felt to her as if she had found the man she never wanted to let go.

Chapter 17

Natalie and Michael left the boat a short time later, hailed a taxi and went to Michael's waterfront home, which wasn't too far away.

The house was stunning to say the least. Natalie was used to opulence having lived with Vance in his ten-thousand-square-foot mansion. But this spectacular home didn't feel empty and cold the way Vance's had. There were personal touches on the walls, such as framed photographs of children's art.

"Aren't these precious?" Natalie commented.

"My nephew and niece drew these pictures," Michael explained. "My niece is a real budding artist. She's nine. Do you believe she drew this picture?" He gestured to the photo of a cat lazing around on the grass.

Natalie walked forward and stared at the picture, her mouth opening in awe. "You're serious? She's only nine?"

Michael nodded. "Yep. The girl is gifted."

"I can't wait to meet her," Natalie said, and then realized the words that came from her lips and what they signified. She was thinking of planning a future with Michael.

Michael's eyes lit up with a smile, one that said he had caught the significance of her words and that he approved. "You'll love her," he said. "Both my niece and nephew."

Natalie would have enjoyed staying longer and checking out the rest of the house. As Michael got dressed and packed a few things for the road, she glimpsed a pool, and a billiards room, but not much else.

"All right," Michael said when he came downstairs with a duffel bag. "To your place?"

"Actually, no." When Michael gave her a questioning look, she explained, "I don't want my sister asking me what I'm doing. We can stop at a store along the way for me to pick up some clothes and other essential items."

"Sure," Michael agreed.

And that's exactly what they did once they were on the Interstate. Seeing a sign for a mall, they pulled off, and Natalie made quick work of buying a couple pairs of jeans, sneakers, sandals, toiletries, some blouses and some shorts.

Then they hit the road.

The drive to the Greater Philadelphia area would take just about seven hours, which meant they were about an hour and a half away from their destination. For most of the drive, Natalie hadn't been in the mood for idle chitchat. She was anxious, Michael could tell. So he had simply tried to assure her with gentle words that they would find her mother, and that she shouldn't stress herself about it.

"God has led you this far," he'd said. "You have to have faith that you'll find her."

"That has been my exact sentiment," Natalie had replied. "But now that we're so close, I'm afraid."

"That's natural. But everything's going to be fine."

He had held her hand as they drove to offer her physical reassurance, but the closer they got to Philadelphia, the more he'd noticed her anxiety. And that was when she'd leaned her head against the window and curled up on the seat, hugged her knees to her chest and closed her eyes. He got the sense that even though he was with her, she was still very much trying to deal with this independently.

Michael had hoped that she would trust him with her thoughts, but maybe this was just her way, so he tried not to let it bother him. As she'd slept, he had taken pleasure from simply looking at her. It felt right having her in this car with him.

In his life.

Michael had never met anyone quite like her before. She was incredibly beautiful, and yet she didn't have the confidence of most beautiful woman. Not that she was insecure, but she was definitely vulnerable. Vulnerable and distrusting.

And it was clear to Michael that the distrust hadn't started simply with her ex-husband. Vance had certainly done a number on her, affecting her negatively, but her distrust had begun when she was younger.

Her mother had abandoned her and her sisters. How did that not affect a person?

Michael only hoped that Natalie would be able to trust him. Yes, she had trusted him enough to share his bed, and their relationship had done a one-eighty from the first time they met. In fact, for Michael, the relationship had progressed at a faster pace than he had ever expected.

He had fallen for her.

Some things were inexplicable, and his feelings for Natalie were inexplicable. All he knew was that he would do anything for her. Something about her made him want to spend the rest of his days protecting her and making her happy.

Michael headed off of the Interstate, and his GPS system began warning him that he had taken a wrong turn.

Natalie opened her eyes and first looked at him, then gazed outside. "We're not there yet?"

"No," Michael said. "I need to stretch my legs, so I'm going to pull into the next gas station. May as well fill up while we're at it."

"Oh. Okay."

A short while later, Michael pulled up to one of the gas pumps and turned off the ignition. Then both he and Natalie exited the vehicle. Natalie stretched her entire body, and Michael couldn't help checking her out. The white shorts she wore amplified the shapeliness of her behind, and her long, sexy legs. He wanted nothing more than to slip his arm around her waist and pull her close.

Yet he had the distinct feeling that if he were to do that, she would reject him. Right now, she needed him in the role of friend, not lover.

"I'm going to head into the store," she said.

"No problem," Michael told her. He lifted the gas nozzle and began to fill the vehicle. He couldn't have been more stunned when, not more than one minute later, Natalie came rushing out of the store looking as though she had seen a ghost.

Michael's eyes widened. "What is it? What's the matter?"

"It's us," she said, her breathing ragged. "You and me."

Michael heard what Natalie was saying, but was so thrown off by the weirdness of her statement that he didn't understand what was going on. Was she taking this moment to tell him that she didn't think they were going to work out?

"You and me," she went on, speaking frantically. "We're on the cover of some tabloid. It says something about me not being too heartbroken over Vance because I've already moved on with you."

"Are you sure?" Michael asked.

"Yes, I'm sure. I just saw it." She seemed mortified. "This is exactly the kind of thing I didn't want to happen. The media following me and you around, spreading salacious stories."

"Someone saw us walking together, took a picture. No big deal."

"It was a picture of the two of us on your yacht," Natalie said.

"Ah." Michael drew in a deep breath. Well, he shouldn't be too surprised. Some reporters did such a good job of lurking behind bushes that you never saw them. It was why he knew that he had to behave publicly in a way that wouldn't embarrass him or his NFL team.

Still, he didn't understand why she seemed so alarmed. "We're seeing each other now," he said. "It's not really that big of a deal if we're photographed together."

Or was it?

"I don't want Vance to see this. Or any of my family."

"Why not?" Michael asked her. "You and Vance are divorced."

Natalie looked at him, but didn't say anything. And Michael felt his heart constrict. When he had first started to pursue her, she had made it clear that she had just gotten out of a relationship, implying that she wasn't ready for a new one. Despite her words, Michael had felt a definite spark of attraction between them, which had encouraged him to try to get to know her better. Everything had been going just as he'd hoped. Now, however, he couldn't help wondering if she had jumped into a relationship with him as a way to distract herself from the pain she was feeling over losing Vance.

Did her heart still belong to her ex?

She wouldn't be the first woman who had been burned by a jerk, only to still carry a torch for him. Maybe she was even blaming herself for Vance's infidelity.

The thing was, Michael had never gotten that sense about Natalie. He hadn't seen her pining over Vance, only the natural distrust as a result of her relationship with him. And the way she had given herself to him in the bedroom…

"I guess…I guess I'm just surprised. Seriously, the one thing I hated about being married to Vance was the fact that the media was so intrusive in our lives. Now that we're divorced, why won't they leave me alone?"

"Let me finish putting gas in the vehicle, then I'll come inside and see the magazine you're talking about."

That seemed to appease her, but she was still on edge. They walked together into the store a short time later, where she surreptitiously pointed out the magazine. And sure enough, there was a picture of the two of them in each other's arms on the deck of the yacht, with the string quartet beside them.

Yeah, a suggestive picture. It couldn't simply have been a shot of the two of them standing side by side.

"It appears that the scorned wife of Vance Cooper, Natalie Hart-Cooper, has moved on has found comfort in the arms of another man just weeks after her divorce," Michael read. "NFL wide receiver Michael Jones is clearly helping her pick up the pieces. But is this lifelong bachelor ready to settle down? Many have tried to tame him. All have failed."

Michael stopped reading and rolled his eyes. He'd seen enough.

"Don't worry about this," he told her. "This is tabloid trash. It may hurt to see it, but it's no big deal. And it's not like you're painted in a bad light. Unlike me."

"I'm not? For one thing, they make it clear that I was only recently married."

"You're divorced. You're allowed to date someone el—"

"*And* they may as well come out and say that they question my judgment in dating another athlete…." She made a sound of derision.

"So you care about the opinion of people you don't even know? Or is this about something else?"

Natalie crossed her arms over her chest. She wouldn't meet his eyes, but she clearly looked uncomfortable.

Michael wondered what the real issue was. Did she just not want Vance to see this? And if not, why not?

"And that bit about you being a lifelong bachelor."

"So some tabloid references my love life, and I'm back to being a player in your eyes?" Michael knew he sounded a little annoyed, but he couldn't help it. He hadn't given Natalie any reason to feel insecure, and she needed to see that.

"Maybe this was a bad idea," she mumbled to herself.

"What was a bad idea?"

"You and me going on this trip together. There'll be more speculation, more—"

"And what exactly is the problem with that?" Michael interjected. "You're not married anymore." He gave her a pointed look. "Or are you still in love with your ex?"

"No," Natalie said.

"Because if you are, you need to tell me."

"No." Natalie stared at Michael, seeing the look of doubt on his face. He wasn't sure he could believe her?

Natalie drew in a deep breath. "We should head back to the car," she said, then went to the door. It made no sense to stand in a gas station store arguing.

After all, who knew how many photographers might be lurking.

She glanced over her shoulder at Michael as he walked out behind her, knowing that there was suddenly tension between them and that it was her fault. If she were honest with herself, she knew that she was the cause of the tension. She had been totally happy to have Michael with her, and then she had been assaulted with doubt. Everything in her life she had hoped for had not worked out.

Why would a relationship with Michael be any different?

She'd married Vance with all the hope in the world, and look what he'd done to her.

Michael *is not* Vance, a voice whispered in her head as he got back into the car.

She looked in Michael's direction. Saw that he didn't look pleased. It hadn't been an off-the-cuff question. He really thought she might still be hung up on Vance.

"I'm sorry," she said as Michael climbed into the car with her. "I saw the picture, and I freaked. It's just that I despise the media and the way they try to capitalize on people's pain. It's not about me and Vance. Not at all."

"All right."

"He and I are over. Forever. And that's how I want it."

"If that's what you're telling me, I have to believe you."

Natalie reached for his hand. "I'm just a little anxious. Here I am, an hour or so away from maybe finding my mother. Suddenly, I'm overwhelmed. I tend to close off emotionally when I'm overwhelmed."

Michael nodded his understanding.

And she was also overwhelmed by what she was feeling for Michael and trying to fight her fear that things would fall apart. She had jumped headlong into a new relationship, and reading that article had her questioning if her actions were wise. She wondered if the follow-your-heart method was the best way to go.

"I'm here with you, and for you," Michael said. Then he squeezed her hand back. "Let's hit the road."

Chapter 18

An hour and a half later, the moment of truth arrived. Michael and Natalie arrived in the North Philadelphia neighborhood where Natalie's mother had once lived.

Natalie stared, her eyes wide and her stomach roiling, a everything around them. Looking at the neglected row house with visible signs of wear and tear, and some even boarded up it was clear that this area of Philadelphia was impoverished

Seeing the house they had come all this way for, the one for which Natalie had the address in a text message from her sister, caused a stab of pain to pierce Natalie's heart. One window was partially boarded up from the inside with either wood or cardboard, and the step's railing was falling to the side. Natalie swallowed. To know that her mother had once lived in such a run-down-looking property was hard to accept

"You okay?" Michael asked.

Natalie shook her head slightly. "I can't believe my mother lived here. It's not like my aunt and uncle had a palace, but

ey lived in a decent neighborhood. Why didn't my mother
ome back to us? To a place that was safer than this?"

"When you see her, you can ask her."

Natalie's heart thumped hard at Michael's statement. Was
he about to get that final clue that would lead her to find her
other? Or—and she knew this was highly unlikely—was
possible that Nigel had gotten it wrong, that her mother in-
eed still lived at this address?

"People are starting to get curious," Michael commented.
As strangers coming into a neighborhood and asking ques-
ions, some people might think we're up to no good. I'm glad
's still light out."

Natalie hadn't thought about that, but as she gazed out at
he street, she noticed two twenty-something women on a
toop a few doors down looking in their direction. A cluster
f teens at one corner was also looking at them. The flashy
Escalade they were in drew a lot of attention in a neighbor-
ood like this.

"We should get out of the car," Michael said. "You ready?"

Natalie sucked in a breath and nodded. "Yep."

Michael opened his car door first, then Natalie did the
ame. As she came around the car to stand beside him,
he couldn't help thinking that this moment was surreal.
he tried to imagine her mother sitting on a stoop and talking
o a girlfriend. Maybe even flirting with someone.

Had she ever thought about them, or had she simply walked
way from them and never looked back?

No, Natalie couldn't believe that. Whatever had happened,
he knew her mother had had a good reason for staying away.
Who would choose to live with strangers here when you could
ive with family in nicer conditions?

Natalie took one step, then another, walking cautiously up
o the door of the dilapidated row house, holding her breath
s she did. She so desperately wanted to find someone here

who could give her answers, and yet this was a total long
shot. But according to Rodney Cook, this was the address
her mother had lived at three years ago, and it was where she
needed to be.

She paused midstep, her eyes taking in everything about
the place. And as she did, the magnitude of everything hit
her then, that her mother had lived in this run-down neighborhood, in a house that was falling apart. She should have
been with them, and instead, she been living on the run like
a criminal. Like a nomad without a proper home.

"Are you okay?" Michael asked.

Natalie expelled the breath she was holding, then gulped
in another one. She shook her head. "My mother lived here.
Look at this place. It's a dump. She suffered through this kind
of an existence while I lived in luxury."

Michael put a hand on her back. "Don't beat yourself up.
It wasn't your choice. It was hers."

"But if she sacrificed to protect us, then how can't I feel
bad?"

"Because you were a child, Natalie. What your mother did
was out of your control. Your mother made some bad choices
and tried to atone for them. Guilt won't accomplish anything
right now. The goal is to find her."

Natalie nodded. "You're right. I know. It just hurts."

Together, Natalie and Michael climbed the steps. After
taking a moment to compose herself, Natalie knocked on
the door.

There was loud hip-hop music blaring inside. Nobody
came to the door, which didn't surprise Natalie. Who could
hear above the music?

But she wouldn't be deterred, and she knocked again.
Pounded, actually. She pounded so hard she was certain that
she would be heard above the music.

Seconds later, the music was turned down.

"Someone's coming," Natalie said, closing her eyes and saying a silent prayer.

The door swung open, and a woman with dreadlocks appeared. She had smooth, dark skin and looked to be in her forties. Her eyebrow rose in question as she looked Natalie up and down, then Michael.

"Yeah?" she said curtly.

"Hi," Natalie began, then swallowed. "My name is Natalie. I'm looking for someone. A woman named Miriam Hart."

"Ain't no one here by that name." The woman looked suspicious. "You all cops?"

"No," Natalie quickly said. "This woman is my mother. I got information that said she used to live here."

"Used to?"

"Yes, but…I was hoping you might know something. It would have been a few years ago that she was here. I'm not sure when she left."

"I don't know no Mary."

"Miriam," Natalie stressed. "Miriam Hart."

"I don't know no Miriam," the woman said, enunciating the name as if to emphasize her point that she didn't know her.

"Like I said, she used to live here before you. I'm wondering if you ever met her, talked to her—"

"I don't know no Miriam," the woman reiterated. "And I don't take too kindly to strangers coming up to my door."

"I'm sorry to just show up like this. It's just…I need to find her."

"I know you're not deaf," the woman snapped. In the background, a child started to wail.

"What about someone named Rodney Cook?" Natalie pressed on.

"I don't know Miriam, I don't know Rodney. Now, I got stuff to do."

They had driven all this way, and Natalie wanted to scream.

All she wanted was something from this woman, something that would lead her in the right direction.

She felt Michael's hand on her shoulder. He was trying to turn her toward him. "Surely you must know something," Natalie said to the woman, her voice wavering.

"Natalie," Michael said.

Natalie faced him. "We've come all this way—"

She stopped short when she heard the door close.

"I can't believe she just did that. She shut the door in my face!"

"Calm down, Natalie," Michael said. "You need to listen to me."

Listen? She wanted to scream and cry and throw something. "We just spend hours driving. I need to find my mother. That woman might know something, even if she doesn't realize that she does."

"And clearly, you're not gonna get through to her. She doesn't know you from Adam."

"This is your idea of support?"

The volume of the music went back up. Natalie pushed herself forward, prepared to pound on the door again, but Michael took her hands before she could.

"Natalie, just listen."

Defiant, she faced him. "So you can tell me that I need to give up, too? Well, I can't."

"The neighbors," Michael said, speaking loudly so that she would hear him.

She went still. "The neighbors?"

"Think about it," Michael went on. "Someone else on this block has probably lived here a long time. They might know your mother. And if not, we can visit community centers tomorrow, food banks, local stores. Someone will have seen her at some point. And that someone can likely point us in the right direction."

Immediately, Natalie felt bad for reacting so defensively. Despite Michael doing everything to support her, she was treating him like the enemy. "I'm sorry. I…I'm just so used to disappointment."

Michael took her by the elbow and led her down the stairs. "I get that. But I've got your back, Natalie, and those aren't words I use lightly."

"I'm sorry," Natalie repeated. And then she moved forward and leaned her forehead against Michael's chest. "I can't believe you haven't run screaming yet."

"From you?"

Natalie raised her head to face him. She nodded. "Maybe I have too many issues."

"We all have our issues. You just have to realize that you're not alone, and that you can trust me."

His words gave her comfort. She knew he was right. And she also knew that for the first time in a long time, she truly felt as if she could trust another human being.

"I do," she said softly. "I do trust you. And I'm so glad you're here. Because I wouldn't have thought about canvassing the neighborhood." A laugh bubbled through her throat, her relief palpable. "Michael, you've given me hope again."

"Someone's got to remember her." He placed his hand on the small of her back. "Let's start going door to door."

So they did. People were definitely curious as to what they were doing, but Michael was cordial with them and no one gave them a problem. In fact, it didn't take long for one guy to recognize him as a professional football player, at which point Michael was surrounded by people looking for autographs.

Michael used the opportunity to his advantage. Once he was finished shaking hands, signing autographs and joking with the few guys who promised that the Eagles would whoop his team, Michael said, "Can any of you tell me if there's someone in this neighborhood, maybe an older woman, who'd

know everything about everything? You know, the one who'
at her window all day and somehow seems to know every
thing that goes on?"

"Miss Dotty," a few people said at the same time, and the
there was a chorus of "yeahs," which made it clear that Mis
Dotty was the woman to talk to.

"Who can tell me where Miss Dotty lives?"

A good dozen people led the way to Miss Dotty's row
house, which was at the end of the block. One of the guy
who'd been particularly chummy with Michael went up the
stairs first and knocked on the door.

Michael put his hand around Natalie's waist. She was feel
ing very confident, and it was all because of him.

It took about a minute, but an older woman who wore he
graying hair in a bun, opened the door.

"Miss Dotty," the fan started, "these folks here would like
to ask you about someone. You been on this block so long,
figure you might be able to help them."

Miss Dotty's eyeglasses were on a string around her neck
and she slipped them on. She looked at Natalie and Michae
with curiosity—and then her eyes lit up. "My heavens. Oh
my word." She clutched her hand to her chest. "You look jus
like her. You must be her daughter."

Overwhelmed with emotion, Natalie couldn't find he
voice. But thankfully, Michael found his. "You know Mir
iam Hart?"

"I know Mary Cardell," the woman said. "And as I live
and breathe, you must be her child!"

Mary Cardell…Miriam Hart. They were similar sounding
names. Her mother had been on the run. It made sense tha
she would use an alias.

For all the good it had done. Rodney Cook had still tracke
her down.

Rodney was out of prison three years ago, on parole, be-

ore getting sent back. He knew where our mother was.... Nat,
think we have to consider the very real possibility that he
ent to Philadelphia, found her and killed her.

"Yes," Natalie said, her breath escaping on a bubbly breath.
he pushed Callie's comment from her mind, because she was
oo close to finding her mother to believe she could be dead.
My name is Natalie. I'm her youngest child."

"Why don't you all come inside?"

"Yes," Natalie agreed. It would be better to have this con-
ersation in the house, away from the curious crowd.

Miss Dotty led them inside, to a small living room with
loral-patterned sofas covered in protective plastic. There
vere all kinds of trinkets adorning shelves and bookcases.
3ut the place was tidy, and homey.

"You are as beautiful as your mother," Miss Dotty said,
eaching up to touch Natalie's face. "Please, have a seat."

Before they did, Michael extended his hand. "I didn't for-
nally introduce myself. I'm Michael."

"And my aren't you handsome? You two make a beauti-
ul couple."

"Thank you, ma'am," Michael said, and sat beside Natalie.

"Where's my mother?" Natalie asked as Miss Dotty low-
red herself onto the armchair.

"Child, I haven't seen your mother in these parts for a good
ouple of months."

A couple of months? Natalie's heart spasmed so hard, she
hought she could have heart failure.

That meant that Rodney couldn't have killed her!

"A couple of months ago," she said, facing Michael, the sig-
ificance hitting her. "That was around when my aunt died."

"She used to live on this block until about three years ago,"
Miss Dotty said. "Then she moved a couple of blocks over,
aying she was trying to avoid someone from her past. I told
er anyone came to bother her, they'd have to get through me.

But she moved nonetheless. Though you wouldn't know it, b
cause she was here all the time. We'd sit and talk and laugh

"Up until a couple of months ago?" Natalie asked, nee
ing to be sure.

"Yes. It was right about then that she said it was time f
her to leave. She said she had to head back to Georgia."

Natalie frowned. "Georgia? Not Ohio?" Maybe her moth
had headed to Ohio for the funeral. But if she had, w
wouldn't she have made her presence known?

"No, she definitely said Georgia."

"Why Georgia? I don't understand."

"When it came to her family business, she was very pr
vate. Didn't say much at all."

"So she has family in Georgia."

"Oh, yes. But she didn't speak about her family. All sh
ever said was that something bad happened to her. In Geo
gia."

Natalie frowned as she pondered the words. Then sh
looked at Michael. "It dawned on me that day of the cooko
that none of my aunt's family was there. They weren't at th
funeral. It made me wonder if both my aunt and my moth
had cut ties with their family. But I asked my uncle, and h
didn't have any answers. Except to say that Auntie Jean didr
talk about her family nor her past."

"Some things are so painful, you want to forget them,
Miss Dotty said.

"And you have no clue what?" Natalie asked.

"I wish I did."

Natalie stood and paced the floor, eyes beginning to mis
"Two months. I missed finding her by two months." Stop
ping, she faced Miss Dotty. "Did she ever talk about me
About her daughters?"

"All the time, child, all the time."

"Then why didn't she ever come back to us? On one hand

'm happy to know that she was alive and well all this time. But that also makes me feel so much pain. Because it means that my mother made a conscious decision not to come back to us."

Miss Dotty stood and approached Natalie. "No. No, child. That's not it."

"Then what?"

"Sometimes, people make decisions they're so ashamed of, they fear no one will be able to forgive them. They fear that those they love are better off without them."

"What are you saying?"

"Your mother...some of the choices she made in her life... especially the ones that put you all in danger...well, she never forgave herself. I tried to convince her otherwise, but her biggest fear was that if she went back for you, you'd reject her."

Natalie's lips parted. "But we...we wouldn't have. We wanted her in our lives."

"Which is what I told her. But she was scared. So she made the decision to love you from afar, rather than take the risk of coming back into your lives, only to find out that you no longer loved her at all."

Chapter 19

Later, as Michael drove away from Miss Dotty's house, Natalie couldn't help pondering the woman's words.

She made the decision to love you from afar, rather than take the risk of coming back into your lives, only to find out that you no longer loved her at all.

The words were somewhat comforting, while at the same time being painful. Because Natalie wished that her mother had never doubted that her daughters would have welcomed her back with open arms.

Sighing softly, she turned to Michael. "I really want to thank you for coming with me. I didn't get the exact answer I wanted, but at least I know more than I did before I got here. It's another piece of the puzzle."

"No problem."

"What you did, it means a lot," Natalie went on. "I appreciate the fact that I didn't have to do this alone."

Michael put his hand on hers and said, "Like I said before

my situation with my mother may not be the same as yours, but I understand what it's like to want something so badly that you do anything to get it. I'd do anything to have my mother well again. To see her walk again. To hear the beautiful voice she used to have. She speaks a little, but her speech is slurred, fragmented." He blew out a breath and shook his head. "If you love your mother even half as much as I love mine…" Michael's words trailed off, and he bit down on his bottom lip as he shook his head.

Natalie's heart ached for Michael. It was clear how deeply he loved his mother. And that yes, he understood her situation. And that he was the kind of man who would support her and her desires.

"Your love for your mother is obvious," Natalie said softly.

"Yeah, she means the world to me," Michael said. "It sucks that there are some things in life out of your control," he added in a whisper.

He was right about that. Natalie had not been able to control her mother's leaving, nor could she control what she was feeling for Michael right now. Because the more time she spent with him, the more she saw how incredible he was. He was truly a different kind of human being than other men.

Michael retraced the path he'd driven into the city, heading back toward the highway. "What's the plan?" Natalie asked. "You planning to head back to Cleveland tonight?"

"I'm happy to drive back to Cleveland tonight, if that's what you want. But there are a lot of good hotels here. Might just be smarter to crash at one and continue with our journey in the morning."

As he met her eyes in the dark car, Natalie felt an electric charge. And just like that, she was ready to put thoughts of the mystery surrounding her mother on the backburner so that she could concentrate on the man she was falling for.

"It's up to you," Michael said when she didn't speak. "I just figured—"

"Sure," she said. "Getting a hotel makes the most sense."

It had been an exhausting day, and when they checked into a hotel half an hour later, they were tired. Given their fatigue, plus the weight of the situation and the conversation they'd had about their mothers, Natalie figured that the only thing on Michael's mind when they stepped into their room would be to get some rest. Her suspicion was confirmed when he gave her a chaste kiss on the forehead and announced that he was going to take a shower.

"Sure," Natalie said. "I'll check out the room-service menu."

He went into the bathroom, and Natalie wandered to the desk, where she found the leather-bound book with the room-service menu. She heard the shower come on as she began perusing the various food items. From burgers to chicken entrées, there was a great selection.

"Hey."

Natalie turned at the sound of Michael's voice. Her eyes widened as she saw his naked torso extended past the door frame, as well as the side of his naked hip and leg. He was strategically positioned to give her an enticing view of his body, without revealing the part she was most interested in seeing.

She swallowed. "Yeah?"

"I was thinking maybe you could join me…help wash my back."

An undeniable jolt of heat passed between them from across the room.

"Long day," Michael said. "We're both sweaty. A nice hot shower for both of us is in order."

Natalie got up and crossed the room to where he stood. She

stopped on the other side of the door frame, allowing him to keep his naked form hidden. "That's all you want? For me to wash your back?"

He framed her face gently, stroking it with his fingers. "Oh, I didn't say that was all."

And then he stepped forward, exposing his fully naked body.

Natalie couldn't stop herself from checking out his beautiful shaft. It was erect, and thick…and it had brought her the most sensual pleasure last night.

Then Michael turned and headed back into the bathroom. "Are you joining me?"

The words sent a thrill through her body, one that had her tingling. She wanted nothing more than to get naked in the shower with him. The sexual tension between them—despite the serious situation and nature of their trip—could not be ignored. What was that about him that turned her on so completely?

So she entered the bathroom. Michael was already in the shower, and she made fast work of stripping out of her clothes. Then she pulled back the shower curtain and stepped into the shower with him.

The water was hot, but not as hot as the look Michael gave her. And then his lips curled in a sly smile, and he took a step toward her. Sweeping her into his arms, he gently kissed her forehead. Natalie moaned. And then Michael's mouth was on hers, but not in the way Natalie would have expected. He kissed her sweetly, an intoxicating kiss that consisted of slow flicks of this tongue and his lips softly playing over hers as the water sluiced over their bodies. And yet the effect was the same as if he was ferociously kissing her, because her body still felt a huge, lustful rush.

She was heady from his kiss. And from the sensation of his naked body pressed against hers.

His hand traveled from her face down the length of he neck and lower, to the area between her breasts. She felt an other rush of heat.

And suddenly, Michael was kissing her more deeply, hi tongue urgently sweeping through her mouth, tantalizing hers. His hands were moving to her hips and he was pulling her upward, against his arousal, making sure she knew jus how much he wanted her.

Needed her was more like it, if the primal sounds coming from his throat were any indication. And it was exactly how she felt, as well. She needed this man. Needed to be naked with him again.

He bent his head, suckled her nipple until she was moaning with pleasure. Then he slipped a hand beneath her thighs and stroked her center, eliciting even more sensual feelings

He pulled back, grinning, while Natalie was breathless Then he picked up the small bar of soap the hotel had provided. "You were going to wash my back."

"I…I…yes." Natalie could hardly speak.

She accepted the bar of soap, lathered it up and ran her soapy hands over his back. She shamelessly checked out his firm behind—then lathered soap over that delectable area of his body.

Michael turned around, and as he took the soap from her hands, his lips sought hers. Then he rubbed it over her torso before moving the small bar up to her breasts.

He tortured her with pleasure, partly lathering her up while also teasing her nipples. As he moved the soap lower down her body, he allowed the water to rinse her breasts, then took one of her nipples into his mouth again.

He suckled her slowly as the water poured over them, as his hands moved the soap to her behind. Natalie wrapped her arms around him and arched her breast into his mouth, enjoying this most erotic shower.

Soon, Michael was dropping the soap, and his hands were roaming all over her, tantalizing her. He kissed her again, deeply, then suckled her bottom lip, driving her wild.

"The bed," he rasped. "Now."

He turned off the shower quickly, then gave Natalie another kiss before he stepped out. He pulled a thick towel off the rack and wrapped it around her before taking one to dry himself.

Natalie patted herself dry, then exited the shower and let the towel fall to the floor. His eyes locked on hers, Michael also dropped his towel. Then he moved toward her, drew her into his arms and lifted her. Sighing softly, Natalie wrapped her legs around him. He held her like that, with her legs around his waist, as he walked out of the bathroom and to the nearby bed. Then he eased down, sitting on the bed first so that her legs were still wrapped around him while her butt was cradled in his lap. A wonderfully sensual thrill shot through Natalie at this erotic position.

Michael broke the kiss and put his lips on the underside of her jaw, thrilling her skin there with the flick of the tip of his tongue. Then he went lower, down her neck, and Natalie purred in response to the exquisite sensations.

"I think you're amazing," Michael rasped. "Beautiful and amazing."

"You're amazing, too. Seriously. I didn't think I would trust anyone again...not so soon."

Michael met her gaze, one eyebrow raised. "You trust me?"

Natalie nodded. "I wouldn't be here with you...like this...if I didn't."

She refrained from telling him that she believed she was feeling a lot more than trust. Everything in her gut told her that she had met the man she would love forever.

Sometimes, you just knew when something was right.

Michael brought his hands to her torso, and she stopped

thinking. She enjoyed the feeling of his palms covering h
skin, his hands covering her breasts, his fingers tweakin
her nipples.

"Oh, yes…"

Michael groaned in response to her utterance of pleasur
and in a flash whipped their bodies around. Now she was o
her back, and he was pressing his lips against her breastbon

"Baby," he whispered, his eyes feasting on her nake
breasts. And then he trailed a finger around each nipple, a
Natalie moaned and arched her back in pleasure.

She felt an explosion of sensation as his mouth came dow
on one nipple. His tongue flicked over her taut peak, brin
ing her to the edge of total bliss.

"I want to take my time pleasing you." His mouth went
her other nipple, and Natalie moaned long and loud.

He kissed a path down to her womanhood, where he ta
talized her with his fingers and his tongue. Minutes late
Natalie was crying out his name as her climax consumed he

"Yes, baby," Michael said, keeping up his pleasurable a
sault until she could no longer stand it.

Natalie couldn't remember ever feeling so incredible. An
once Michael slipped on a condom, settled between her thigl
and thrust into her…she felt a sense of completion that wer
far beyond the physical.

As Michael took his time with her, made sweet love
her, Natalie knew that what she felt in her heart for him wa
definitely love.

Chapter 20

When the night of the auction rolled around, Natalie was still on an emotional high. The lead concerning her mother put her in positive spirits. As did her relationship with Michael.

She never would have thought it possible, but she had definitely fallen for him.

She hadn't seen him in a few days, and he dealt with some preseason business, so when they got together for the auction, she was especially excited to see him. They shared a steamy kiss before they took the stage to host.

Their banter as hosts was easy, light and humorous, and seemed to please the crowd. Penelope was all smiles as the night went on.

"And now," Natalie began, "the part of the night that all of the women have been waiting for." She glanced at Michael, gave him a little wink that she hoped no one else would notice. "We are about to start the bidding for an evening with Michael Jones!"

The bidding started at one hundred dollars, and within couple of minutes, it became clear that there were three s rious contenders. But once the bidding got to two thousan dollars, one of the women backed out, leaving only two.

"Five thousand dollars," one of the two women called ou with a determination that said she would not be denied a evening with Michael.

An excited hum spread through the crowd. And then som people began to clap. The other woman who had been bic ding laid her paddle on the table and shrugged.

"Going once," Natalie said. "Going twice." She pause waited. "Sold to number fourteen for five thousand dollars!

And as the woman leaped to her feet, jumping excitedl it struck Natalie for the first time that she looked familia *Yes, of course she does. She's the fan who approached M chael at his yacht.*

And she had a niggling sensation then, one that told he perhaps something was wrong.

But when she mentioned the coincidence to Michael late he merely shrugged. "Yeah, I guess you're right."

"I can't imagine where Michael would be," Penelope sai the next afternoon as Natalie sat with her in the charity's o fice. "I was hoping you would both be here for this meeting.

Natalie hadn't been able to reach him either this mornin, but she had spent the night with him. "He said he needed t see his mother."

"Yes," Penelope said, tsking softly. "He mentioned her ac cident, and that she's in a special home."

"Hopefully there's been no setback with her health."

"I hope not," Penelope concurred. After a moment, sh said, "Well, I suppose I should get to the point of the mee ing. The fundraiser was *fantastic!* We raised a staggerin amount of money. Well into six figures. I'm so pleased that I chose you and Michael for this."

"I'm thrilled that I could be a part of it."

"Since Michael isn't here," Penelope went on, "I'll give you this now." She reached into her desk and produced a small, gift-wrapped package. "Here."

Smiling, Natalie accepted the gift and opened the silver foil. Inside was a gold pin with the Compassion For Families emblem, which consisted of two children holding the hands of a female in the center.

"This is lovely," Natalie said. "I'll cherish it always."

"And…" Penelope went on, grinning widely. "There's also this."

Penelope passed her an envelope, and when Natalie opened it, she saw a gift certificate to a popular shop in town that sold a variety of items, from clothes to jewelry to perfume. "This wasn't necessary. I'd rather you keep the money for the charity."

"The store graciously donated these gifts. One for you, and one for Michael."

"In that case, thank you. Like I said, I'm honored to have been a part of this."

Natalie and Penelope concluded their meeting, and feeling a sense of pride, Natalie left the building.

She was on her way to her car when she heard someone call her name. Stopping, Natalie glanced over her shoulder.

"Mrs. Cooper." The woman smiled brightly.

For some reason, Natalie's stomach lurched. It was the woman who had won the auction for the date with Michael. The same one who had been outside his yacht.

"Natalie," Natalie corrected. "And your name is Leanne, right?"

"Yes," Leanne said. "So you remember me."

"Of course."

Leanne walked closer to her. "I just wanted to thank you personally for the fundraiser."

"Oh. Do you have a child or know someone with a child who is suffering from a life-threatening illness?" Perhaps that explained why the woman had so vigorously bid on Michael for a date, and why she was here outside of the charity.

Leanne shook her head. "No, not that. I wanted to thank you for the auction with Michael." She smiled sheepishly. "We talked this morning about the date, and we met for lunch. The great news is that now our relationship is back on track."

Natalie stared at Leanne as if she had turned into a martian. "What? What did you say?"

"Oh, my. I hope you're okay," Leanne said. "I mean, you *did* know, didn't you? That Michael and I had been involved."

Relationship back on track. Involved. Natalie suddenly found it hard to suck in air.

"Oh, my God. He didn't tell you. I just assumed...that day I saw you at the yacht..."

"The day I saw you at the yacht you pretended to be a fan."

Leanne shrugged. "Well, that is true. I was trying to determine what the nature of your relationship was. I admit, I wasn't forthright."

"Michael was angry," Natalie went on.

"He was shocked to see me. We'd been having problems, and we broke up. Obviously, he was interested in you. But as he said to me this morning, he doesn't believe you're over your husband."

"This is ridiculous," Natalie said, and started toward her car.

"Is it?" Leanne asked. "Do you doubt I was with Michael this morning?"

And with that question, Natalie began to doubt. She hadn't been able to reach Michael. *Why not?*

Was it at all possible this woman was telling the truth?

"I can see you're having trouble digesting what I'm telling you," Leanne went on. "Maybe this will help you believe. Michael has a scar. About two inches long, on the right side of his back."

Natalie's stomach felt as if it had just bottomed out. She had seen that scar on his back when they were in the shower.

"For what it's worth," Leanne went on, "you and Michael weren't going to work out. He was on the rebound from me, just like you're on the rebound from Vance."

Natalie couldn't stand to hear any more, so she quickly hurried off and got into the safety of her car.

She sat there, her breathing labored, digesting what had happened.

And she came to the one conclusion that was certain. Michael had lied to her.

The same as Vance had.

Chapter 21

For the next two days, Natalie didn't return Michael's calls. She was back to being angry.

Angry that she had been duped by him. Angry that she had let her guard down. Angry that she had shared her body with him.

That she had fallen for him.

Her sisters had encouraged her to talk to Michael, to hear his explanation about Leanne, because as Deanna said, the woman sounded "hinky."

That was true enough, but it was obvious that this Leanne woman had had a relationship with him.

Something Michael had deliberately not told her.

If he couldn't be honest with her, then how could she trust him?

In his voice messages and texts, he had expressed confusion as to why she wasn't getting back to him. But he knew he had lied to her. By now he should have figured out why she wasn't talking to him.

On the third day, if only to give Michael a piece of her mind because her heart was hurting so badly, Natalie answered his call. "Hello?" she said tersely.

"What's going on?" Michael asked without preamble.

Perhaps it was best to have this conversation in person, but the truth was, she didn't want to see him. It would be too hard, because her heart still cared for him. She couldn't easily shut her feelings off. The best she could do was make sure to keep her distance.

"I talked to Leanne," Natalie said. "I know all about the two of you."

Silence filled her ear, and Natalie shook her head in disgust. "I see you have nothing to say."

Michael heaved a heavy sigh. "Nothing is going on with me and Leanne."

"At least now you're admitting that you know her. Something you should have done a long time ago."

"The woman is crazy. She's been following me around, stalking me."

"You're telling me you've never had a relationship with her?"

A beat. "Not exactly."

"Nice."

"But it isn't what you think," Michael quickly said. "It didn't get serious. We went out a couple of times, and I quickly learned that she was a gold digger."

"She knows that you have a scar on your back!" Natalie countered.

"You think I slept with her?"

Natalie didn't answer, but that was exactly what she was thinking. "If it was before your relationship with me, you

don't have to lie about it. The fact that you are makes m
distrust you."

"Leanne could have been spying on me through my win
dow with binoculars for all I know. I've been seen withou
my shirt on in public many times. Photographed that way. /
lot of people know about that scar."

"Where were you the day after the fundraiser?" Natali
asked. "Neither Penelope nor I could reach you. Leanne say
you met with her."

"Damn it," Michael muttered.

"Ah, so you did."

"No, I didn't *meet* with her. She came up to me at the en
of the fundraiser, told me how excited she was about our date
That's when I told her I *wouldn't* be going out with her. That
would make sure I paid the five thousand dollars to the char
ity on her behalf. She wasn't happy, but I thought that wa
the end of it. The next morning, I went to visit my mother
As I left the home, Leanne was by my car, waiting for me
She did her best to tell me that we needed to be together, an
I blew her off."

"And that's why you didn't answer your phone?" Natali
asked doubtfully. Had Michael had his body wrapped around
Leanne's in his bed?

"I didn't answer the phone because shortly after I left my
mother, I got a call saying she was being rushed to the hos
pital. She was having a seizure, they thought it could hav
been a stroke. Thank God it wasn't a stroke, but it was a long
and hectic day. I called to tell you about it that evening. You
didn't answer the phone."

Natalie hesitated. His story had the ring of truth. And from
everything she knew of Michael, he wasn't the type to use
his ill mother as an alibi.

But could she trust her heart and her gut where any man
was concerned?

"I went out with Leanne a year ago, and I'm telling you, I wish I hadn't. I thought then that her being a gold digger was the worst of it. Man, was I ever wrong. Obviously she decided her next best option to win my love would be to try to ruin what I have with you."

"Why didn't you call her out on her charade at the yacht, then?" Natalie questioned. She continued before Michael could answer. "Because you didn't want me to know the truth."

"Because I didn't want you to jump to the wrong conclusion."

"Easy to say now. But you still lied."

"This is exactly why I didn't want to tell you," Michael said. "Because I knew that you would become suspicious. See me as a cheating dog because of your experience with Vance."

Natalie scoffed. "And you're not?"

"Wow," he said. "I thought that what we shared…it would show you… Wow."

Natalie's heart felt as though someone had put it in a vise. She was just so confused. Michael seemed earnest.

But then, so had Vance.

"All I know right now is that I got involved with you way too quickly," Natalie said. "I'm not sure of anything anymore."

"So you're going to walk away from me?"

"Yes," Natalie said with difficulty. "I made it clear to you that I needed honesty. If you couldn't tell me the truth about someone like Leanne, how can I trust that you'll tell me the truth about anything else? Obviously, you won't have any trouble finding someone to take my place."

"Our relationship was insignificant to you? That's what you're saying?"

"This is your doing, Michael. Because you weren't honest!"

"If you can walk away from me right now, even though

I've explained the situation, then it seems to me that you were looking for the first excuse to justify bolting. Leanne handed you that on a silver platter."

"This is about honesty," Natalie reiterated. "You need to understand that."

"Honesty and trust works both ways."

"I haven't given you a reason not to trust me," Natalie said.

"Really? The fact that you would so easily take the word of a psycho and not me? The fact that you're not invested in this relationship after I've poured my heart out to you? You're a gorgeous woman," he continued. "Clearly desired by many men. You might be afraid that I'm the one who will chase the first skirt that walks by, but women cheat, too. There are no guarantees that you'll be faithful to me."

Natalie said nothing.

"After all, it was your friend who cheated with your husband. A woman did that. I know men can behave badly, and yeah, there are a lot of dogs in the world of professional sports. But the women chasing those men trying to get knocked up or ruin happy homes just to have a piece of the pie are no better than the men who are willing to sleep with them. Remember that."

"She knew where your yacht was—"

"Because she's been stalking me! I told you that already."

"So you say," Natalie retorted, and all she could think of was how much it had hurt to learn that Vance had been cheating on her. She didn't want to be a fool a second time.

"For God's sake."

"Look, you're angry with me, I'm angry with you," Natalie said. "I guess we go our separate ways and that's it."

"Were you ever invested in us?" Michael countered. "Or maybe you'll never be able to trust anyone, because of the issues surrounding your mother's abandonment."

Natalie opened her mouth to speak, but she said nothing.

His comment touched a nerve, because she knew he was right. After spending so much of her life wanting to trust—to trust that her mother would come back, to trust that men wouldn't hurt her—she *did* have a hard time putting her faith in people now. Her sisters had so often said that she was the one who wanted to believe in fairy tales, and that had been true—but time and time again, her faith that people would do the right thing had only proven her gullibility.

"You're making me pay for Vance's mistakes. And that's wrong."

Natalie hung up. Because she couldn't stand to hear another word Michael had to say.

Or maybe the truth was that she couldn't stand to hear him point out so accurately what her issues were. Because how could she go back to being the woman who believed in fairy tales—and allow herself to get hurt again?

And then she started to cry, because she already *was* hurt. She had already started to believe in the fairy tale with Michael.

And now she was walking away from it.

The next few days passed with no call from Michael. And though Natalie had told him that they were over, she felt a sense of disappointment when she didn't see his number on her phone whenever it rang.

Today, though, she felt an immediate tightening sensation in her chest when her phone rang. Because Vance's number was displayed on her screen.

Why was he calling her? And after all this time?

She didn't answer the phone. She didn't want to talk to him. But no sooner than the ringing stopped, it began again. And she realized that he would probably call until he got through to her. So she answered the phone and put it to her ear saying tentatively, "Hello?"

"Nat," Vance responded. "I'm glad you answered."

"What do you want?" she asked.

"I need to see you."

"I have no clue why. Surely you can't want me to take part in your wedding," she added sourly.

"That's just it," he said. "There isn't going to be a wedding."

Natalie had no clue what to say to that. So she said nothing.

"Are you there?"

"I'm here," she responded tersely. "So, your relationship is falling apart and suddenly you're calling me?"

"Olivia lied to me. She's not pregnant."

"I don't see how that's my problem."

"We were married," Vance went on softly. "And I have no excuse for what I did. But all I can tell you is that without you in my life, things aren't right."

"Not my problem."

"Do you want me to grovel? Because I'll head to Cleveland and grovel."

"I don't want you to grovel."

"Then please at least accept my apology." He paused. "Listen, babe. I realize now just how much I love you. I always knew it. I was just… I was stupid. I'm begging you to forgive me."

Natalie didn't speak.

"How about we get together for dinner? To talk."

"But you're—" The words died on her lips. Suddenly she realized that Vance must be in town.

"Go to your front door," he said, and she could hear a smile in his voice.

Natalie's heart began to pound as she walked downstairs from her bedroom and looked through the side window at the front door. And then she gasped. There were countless bouquets of bright red roses on the porch step.

She opened the door and stepped outside, taking inventory. That's when Vance stepped from the side of the house and into view. In the hand that wasn't holding the phone, he held a single red rose.

"Hey," he said softly.

"What are you—what are you doing?" Natalie sputtered.

"Have dinner with me," he said. He slipped his cell phone into the pocket of his black slacks. "I know these roses can't make up for what I did. Because my cheating was unforgivable." He climbed the stairs. "Trust me, I've been talking to my pastor, trying to clear my conscience and understand why I did some of the things I did. My father wasn't in my life, my mother was always off with a different boyfriend. Let me take you to dinner. We can share a bottle of wine and really talk."

Was he out of his mind? "I can't go to dinner with you, Vance."

Vance nodded. "Okay. I can respect that. Then let me tell you face-to-face just how sorry I am. I hope that one day you can find it in your heart to forgive me. And if there's ever a chance we can work things out…I'd love that opportunity. But what I really hope is that we can forge some sort of relationship. I want you in my life, if only as a friend."

Friends? Was he serious?

Surprisingly, he looked it.

"Vance," Natalie began, then stopped. She drew in a breath and considered her words. "I'm not sure what compelled you to come all the way here to talk to me, but if you're truly sorry, then I accept your apology. As for being friends… I don't know. Maybe one day. But not right now. Not after everything."

Vance nodded again, and Natalie was surprised that he seemed so agreeable. Maybe he had been getting some sort of counseling as well as religious advice.

"I'll be in town for a few more days," he said. "If you're

willing to get together, will you call me? You know my cell number." Vance started down the steps. "Okay, maybe too much to ask."

Natalie was flabbergasted. And she certainly wasn't about to call him. Not in this lifetime.

But something else became clear to her as she watched Vance get into a car parked at the curb. After divorcing her without even giving her the courtesy of a phone call, seeing Vance now had given her a sense of closure.

And that was all she truly wanted from him.

Chapter 22

Michael felt like crap. Natalie had walked out of his life. Days after their conversation—despite his explanation about Leanne—she hadn't reached out to him.

And it hurt.

He hadn't expected to fall for her so deeply, but the intensity of his painful feelings made it clear that that's exactly what had happened.

He still remembered the look on her face when she came out of his friend's store in her stunning designer dress—God, that dress—and the smile that lit up on her face when she saw the limousine. She had accused him on more than one occasion of having the kind of money that made it easy to pull off grand gestures. And yes, that was true. But he had never done that kind of thing for a woman before because he had never been compelled to.

She had compelled him to plan their extravagant romantic evening. And what she didn't seem to understand was that it wasn't easy because of the money, but because of what was in his heart.

He had told her in no uncertain terms that she was making him pay for Vance's mistakes. He had hoped that his words would have an effect on her, make her realize that he was absolutely right. But in the days that had passed since their argument, it became clear Natalie wasn't going to call him.

And Michael didn't know what to do with himself. Because all he could remember was the soft feel of her body against his, those purring sounds she made that drove him wild. How much he had needed to please her in a way he never felt the need to please another woman before.

He finally understood what giving and receiving love was supposed to feel like. Because he hadn't seen it with his own family, and hell, the guys around him certainly didn't practice it.

But he could chase Natalie all he wanted, wow her with more grand gestures as she called them, but if she didn't trust him… She needed to learn to trust him, or nothing would ever change.

And that was what he was afraid of. That she would never learn that. No amount of calls to her or explanations on his part would persuade her of something she didn't believe in her own heart.

Michael, who was lounging on the leather sofa in his rec room, decided to surf the Net. He went to the computer and opened a web browser.

News stories always were the first items to fill the browser's screen, stories Michael typically ignored.

But not this time.

This time, he stared at the photograph of Natalie and Vance standing on a front porch covered in bouquets of red roses. The headline read, Vance Cooper and his Jilted Wife Reunite.

And suddenly, Michael knew what was really going on. Why Natalie had rejected him.

Natalie entered the kitchen to the wide-eyed stares of Deanna and her uncle. She looked at each in turn, noted that yes, they were looking at her with curiosity, and she wondered what had happened from last night until this morning.

"Good morning… I think." She paused, frowning. "What's up?"

"Now I know it's not any of my business," her uncle began, "but I would think that after the way Vance treated you, you would not run back to him like some fool."

Natalie's eyebrows shot up. "Excuse me?"

"He can send all the flowers here he wants, that doesn't change his moral character," Uncle Dave huffed. "My goodness, that man has the moral fiber of a cockroach."

Natalie sat at the table between her uncle and her sister. "What are you talking about?"

"There's a picture on the front page of the newspaper," Deanna explained, sounding grave. "It shows you and Vance—*here,* yesterday. And the caption says that the two of you are getting back together."

"What?" Natalie all but shrieked.

Deanna lifted the paper, which had been on her lap, and put it onto the table.

Natalie cringed. The photo showed her and Vance standing close together, and they looked as if they were having an intimate conversation. Even more damning was the single rose Vance was holding, extending to her.

"H-how?" Natalie questioned, wondering who had taken this photo.

"Uncle Dave is confused, and so am I," Deanna said. "But I figure you had a good reason for meeting with Vance and not telling us."

"He came by when you and Uncle Dave were at the movies." Natalie hadn't been in the mood to go so she'd stayed home. "I didn't tell you because I didn't think it was important."

"Of course, it's totally your choice what you do," Deanna said. "But we were surprised, is all. I didn't think you would give him the time of day."

"What I don't understand is why this is in the paper," Natalie commented. "Some reporter was lurking, ready to get this damning shot?" Lord, how she despised not being able to have her privacy anymore.

"Vance obviously talked to the reporter," Deanna said. "He's quoted as saying you two are working out your problems."

Natalie's eyes widened. "He said that? *No*—we are *not* getting back together. He showed up here, said he wanted to apologize, and hoped that one day I could forgive—" Natalie stopped abruptly, suddenly thinking of Michael. "Oh, my God."

If Michael saw this…

Suddenly, she was panicked. She didn't want Michael to see this, see the picture of her and Vance and come to the conclusion that her family had come to. She knew how it would look, but appearances were not as they seemed.

"Oh, God," Natalie uttered. "I have to talk to Michael."

It was early, but she jumped up from the table nonetheless and ran upstairs. She found her phone and dialed his number. But he didn't answer.

When she tried two more times and he still didn't answer, Natalie did the only other thing she could. She got dressed and rushed out of the house.

Because the idea that Michael would see this article and think that she and Vance were getting back together was terrifying to her.

She drove to his house as quickly as she could, leaped out of her car and ran up his front steps. Then she rang the doorbell and also knocked on the door. When he didn't answer within a minute, she began to pound.

Finally, she saw him approaching the door through the paneled glass, and relief washed over her. But when he opened the door and looked at her with a dismal expression, it was clear that he'd seen the paper.

"We need to talk," Natalie said. "Can I come in?"

"We don't need to talk. I finally understand."

Natalie's heart sank. "No, you don't understand. What was reported in the paper…it's not true. I don't even know how anyone got that picture."

"The one with you, Vance and the rose at your uncle's house?"

"He showed up with roses, but…but what the paper said was wrong. Vance and I are *not* getting back together."

"Why are you here? Why are you telling me this?"

Natalie's mouth fell open at his question.

She hadn't thought of anything but getting to him and doing damage control…before it was too late.

"Because…" she said. *Because I love you.*

"It's okay," Michael said. "Seeing that picture of you and Vance made it clear to me that as much as I've been chasing you, you were never that interested."

"You're wrong."

"You used the word of an obsessed woman to dump me, despite me explaining the way things really were. Yet the man who treated you with so little respect comes to town and tries to woo you and you don't hesitate to give him the time of day. It was a wake-up call for me. I'm not sure your heart was ever free to give."

Hearing Michael say those words was devastating. "No.

You're wrong. I'm over Vance. Seeing him made me truly realize that he is out of my heart."

"I played this game once before. With someone in college. We started dating, but she broke up with the guy she really loved not that long before. Turned out I was just the rebound guy for her. That guy came back, and no, she didn't take him back right away, but ultimately she did."

"That's not going to happen with me," Natalie said.

"What are you saying?" Michael held her gaze, a challenge in his eyes.

"I'm saying..." Natalie sighed softly, then knew she had to lay it all on the line. "I'm trying to say that I'm here because I don't want to lose you. I know, I pushed you away, but seeing the article made me realize that you would see it, and that you might get the wrong idea and never want anything to do with me. And I...I couldn't stand that. I want you back, Michael."

"How can I be sure? How can I put my heart on the line only for you to crush it? Because what I feel for you is stronger than you realize."

Natalie's chest heaved. And then she got the meaning of what Michael was saying.

"Trust goes both ways," Michael said softly.

"You're right," Natalie said. "And I get it. I chastised you because of what Leanne said, and you can easily do the same to me. Because the way things appear, why wouldn't you think that Vance and I are getting back together?"

"Exactly."

Natalie stepped forward. "You said something when we last spoke that is definitely true. My issues with trust started long before Vance. They started with my mother." She took a deep breath. "But one other thing is absolutely true." She placed a hand on his chest. "I *know* I can trust you, Michael, in a way I never knew I could trust Vance. I was just..."

just scared. Scared of making another mistake. Every day I wanted to call you. Every day I've missed you. But seeing the article about me and Vance terrified me. Terrified me because I thought you might write me off forever."

"*You* wrote me off."

"I know. I know it seems that way. But no matter how much I told myself to forget you, I couldn't make myself stop loving you."

First, Michael's lips parted. And then one of his eyebrows arched. Finally, Natalie saw the slightest hint of a smile on his lips.

"You love me?" he asked.

The admission was liberating. "Yes." A long breath oozed out of her. "I fell in love with you the night you took me out on your yacht."

Now Michael's smile widened. "That's the night I fell in love with you, too."

"You did?"

Michael nodded. "Yeah. I did."

"I'm sorry," Natalie said. "I really am. I hope you can believe me."

"You willing to come inside and prove it to me?" he asked, his tone playful.

Natalie raised an eyebrow, a wave of heat washing over her. "How can I prove it to you?" Natalie asked, her voice husky.

"Oh, I think you can figure something out."

"Yeah," Natalie agreed. "I think I can."

"Then come here," Michael growled, and pulled her into his arms.

Natalie grinned from ear to ear. And then Michael's mouth came down onto hers, and heat spread through her entire body.

But most important was the feeling of love that filled her heart.

She had almost let this incredible man walk out of her life forever. But now that he was back in her arms, she would never let him go.

* * * * *

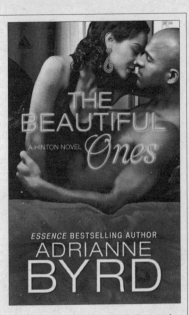

 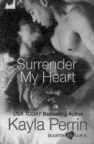 

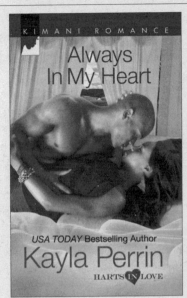

For lovers only...

REQUEST YOUR FREE BOOKS!

2 FREE NOVELS
PLUS 2 *FREE GIFTS!*

KIMANI™ ROMANCE

Love's ultimate destination!

A Brand-New Madaris Family Novel!

NEW YORK TIMES BESTSELLING AUTHOR

BRENDA JACKSON

COURTING JUSTICE

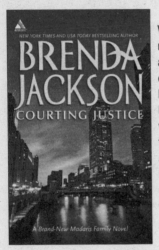

Winning a high-profile case may have helped New York attorney DeAngelo DiMeglio's career, but it hasn't helped him win the woman he loves. Peyton Mahoney doesn't want anything more than a fling with DeAngelo. Until another high-profile case brings them to opposing sides of the courtroom…and then their sizzling attraction can no longer be denied.

"Brenda Jackson is the queen of newly discovered love, especially in her Madaris Family series."
—*BookPage* on *Inseparable*

Available May 29, 2012, wherever books are sold.

KIMANI PRESS™
www.kimanipress.com